Kristina Beck

Colors and Curves

Colors and Curves

ISBN: 978-3-947985-12-8

To Aunt Marcie

1

SKYLAR

I laughed when my family warned me that summer in New York City could be unbearable at times. I mean, I've lived in Boston most of my life—how could New York be that much different? Well, let me tell you, I've been wearing the least amount of clothes possible without being arrested for streaking. The sweltering heat and heavy humidity has practically melted the skyscrapers. The Amazon rainforest probably feels like an icebox compared to here. Until last night anyway. Spectacular thunderstorms blew through the city, bringing with them an awesome show of lightning. All that sucked the humidity right out. It's still crazy hot, but at least the air is breathable again—so much so that I've decided to venture out to Central Park.

Apparently, I'm not the only one with that plan. The sidewalks are packed, and people keep bumping into me. A refreshing droplet of condensation from my giant Dunkin' iced coffee slides down my narrow cleavage as I hold my drink close to my chest like an old woman clutches her purse. I asked for three extra shots of espresso. It was probably not the best choice after the week I've had. If I'm not careful, I'll be breakdancing through the park instead of walking. I suck down a huge gulp and cringe at the resulting brain freeze. Will I ever learn when I drink these damn things?

In the distance, the swaying branches of my favorite big willow tree wave to me gracefully. It's like being greeted by an old friend after a long day of work at the gallery. I can't wait to sit down and relax against its supportive trunk.

"Chance! Heel!" A loud male voice catches my attention. I turn around to see a three-legged dog dragging a long leash and zigzagging wildly after a skittish squirrel, a cloud of dust following behind. Oh, shit! They're heading my way. At the last second, the squirrel swerves to the right and scrambles up a tree. The dog doesn't have time to adjust its path, and I don't have time to move. Suddenly, I'm tumbling backward and watching my coffee as it slips from my hand into a messy freefall. My ass hits the ground hard and, next thing I know, I'm flat on my back. For a moment, I'm numb, until I'm shocked back to reality by a rough tongue licking my chest and face. What in the ever-loving fuck? As I sit up, the dog's rough paw gets lodged in the top of my strapless sundress. I grab the edge of it just in time to keep my boobs from flying out.

"Chance! What the hell has gotten into you? Get off her!" The dog gets in one more lick before his weight lifts off me.

I push my hair out of my face and feel a breeze

between my legs. *Oh no*. I glance down and get a glimpse of my red lace underwear on display like the photographs in the gallery. Faster than I can think, my hand grabs the bottom of my dress and stuffs it between my legs. I don't embarrass easily, but I'm pretty sure the color of my face is currently matching my underwear.

"Are you okay?" His voice is cold and gruff, almost like he doesn't care and is more annoyed than anything. Yet it sends pleasant shivers down my spine. Why?

"Yeah. I think—" I stop to take inventory. My arms and legs look fine, but I touch my chest because it stings. When I pull my hand away, it's slightly wet and sticky. I look down, expecting it to be dog slime or coffee, but instead, it's blood. "No way! I'm bleeding. Shit!"

My handbag is next to me on the ground, covered in coffee. *That figures.* I grab a pack of tissues and use one to blot my chest. I pull it away to find a small dot of blood. *Phew.* Nothing major. I'm supposed to wear a strapless dress to the opening on Friday night.

"Where? I don't see anything." *Are you kidding me?* Did he not see me wiping it off with the tissue? Can't he at least pretend to care?

"What the hell do you think this is?" I point to my chest. "If you don't see the scratch right here and the blood on this tissue"—I hold it out so he can see—"then you must be blind."

He snorts, and I lift my angry gaze to meet the most unique brown eyes. Deep reddish-brown like redwood or cognac. Fiery. Beautiful. *Whoa.* What was I saying? I've lost all train of thought. I'm suddenly envisioning him coming out of a burning house with only his fireman suspender pants on, muscles tight and slick, with a hose hanging over his shoulder and a puppy in one hand. *Puppy?*

Sluurp! Well, that's a guaranteed way to kill a fantasy… unless it's the guy's tongue. And this wasn't.

"Can you please keep your dog off me? I like dogs, but this is fucking ridiculous."

"Then get off the ground," he snidely remarks, tugging gently on the leash.

Oooh, really? "Who pissed in your damn Cheerios this morning? I'm the one who's bleeding and covered with dirt and coffee here." I grab more tissues and wipe the coffee from my bag and legs. It's on my dress too. This had better not stain! What a waste of coffee money.

The jerk crosses his arms, revealing toned biceps. I can't help but notice the dog—Chance?—as he winds himself around the guy's long, muscular legs. Why is he still standing here if he doesn't intend to speak to me? We should part ways and call it a day.

I don't care how chiseled his jaw is or that the wind just blew the heavenly scent of male sweat and soap my way or that there's a hint of ink peeking around from his shoulder and neck… Nope. He might look like a god, but he's nothing more than a prick on a stick or a devil in disguise. I lock my jaw into place, like his. The jerk hasn't even offered to help me up. I don't need his damn help anyway.

I push off the ground with the least amount of grace. Finally on my feet, I brush my hands down my flowy, floral dress. "Dogs should always be on a leash, you know," I say. Ugh—why bother with the dress. It's covered in dirt, dog spit, and coffee.

The dog in question is unwinding himself like it's the most fun he's ever had. If only life could be so easy. He's adorable and I want to take him home with me.

"Look, it wasn't my fault. He took off after a squirrel, and the leash snapped. I can't help it if you were suddenly more enticing than the squirrel." His voice has a twang of disgust, but I watch as he checks me out. His cold, squinted eyes slowly defrost, and I catch the exact second when he zones in on my breasts. *Typical asshole.*

My defenses kick in, but at the same time, I realize I've been doing the same thing to him. Then I'm pissed because I like how he's looking at them… at me. Like he's branding me as his. *Stop!* I cross my arms over my chest, mirroring his stance. We look like we're about to face off.

Maybe he was just looking at the scratch. *Nah.* My track record with men says no. "What are you looking at? Eyes up here." I snap my fingers.

The dog sits pretty and looks at me with his tongue dangling out. I almost laugh. "Not you, little boy. I'm talking about your owner over here." I am not going to stoop to his level and ask what the jerk's name is.

I look up and lock eyes with the guy again. He tips his head to the side and twists his lips into a slight curve. Is that a smile?

Whatever it is, it sends pleasant shivers down my spine… again! Can he stop making himself look so damn sexy? His eyes are hypnotic, and his delicious lips beg me to kiss them.

"Where Chance had his paw."

"What?""

"I'm looking at your chest. I mean the scratch."

Yeah, which is it—my chest or the scratch? Those are two very different things. I'm not going to pursue it. I should just walk away, but I can't deny the pull I feel toward him.

I roll my eyes. "Maybe you should invest in a stronger leash. Aren't you at least going to apologize for your dog?"

His squinted eyes come out of their trance, his back straightens, and I suddenly realize how tall he is. I'm five eight, and I'd guess he's probably five or six inches taller. *Yummy.* He removes the sunglasses hanging from his tank top, then puts them on.

"Fine. I'm sorry."

"*Pfft!* That was the worst apology I've ever heard. At least try to sound like you mean it." Drop-dead gorgeous or not, he's just more proof… All men suck!

The dog licks my hand as if he's the one apologizing. I kneel down and scratch behind his droopy ears. "Your name is Chance, right?" I coo. "You sure do know how to run with only three legs. You have better manners than your human." He barks in agreement.

The guy snickers. "Gee, thanks, Chance. Man's best friend. Yeah, right."

He has to be the cutest dog ever. Just like his owner. He's spotted, black and white, maybe a Beagle mix. One eye is powder blue and the other is brown. I can't help but notice the similarities between him and his owner, who has black hair, brown eyes, and is wearing black and white Nike track shorts and a tank top.

Ignoring me, the man picks up the broken leash. "Chance, leave her alone, buddy. Let's go."

I guess he's only nice to his dog. He rolls over and exposes his belly. The dog, not the prick on a stick. The *dog* just won my heart, not his jackass owner… no matter how hot he is.

Nope. I should run away from him as fast as I can.

2

JULIUS

"Chance, leave her alone, buddy. Let's go," I say, tugging on his leash. Instead, he flops down, and the woman reaches out—*No, don't do it! Don't!* Too late. She tucks her dress behind her knees and crouches to rub his belly. I scratch the back of my neck and sigh. He's not going to budge while she's doing that. Belly rubs are like a drug to him. Now she'll be his best friend. *Not good.*

I saw her before Chance ran her over. It was like sunbeams were shining down on her, spotlighting her through dense clouds, even though the sky was crystal clear. Her aura radiated a bright light that pulled me in like a magnet. I had to squint against her brilliance even with my sunglasses on. Her hair and dress blew softly in the breeze. Truly, I thought she was an illusion. But then, I don't know—did Chance feel it too? He so suddenly lost interest in that squirrel and ran for her instead.

And when I got closer, I had to take my sunglasses

off to see if her skin really shimmered like she'd been dipped in sparkles. I'm embarrassed to admit it, but it was like… remember that scene in *Twilight,* when what's-his-face revealed his skin in the sun? That's what flashed before my eyes. And no, I'm not a *Twilight* fan, and no, I don't think this woman's a vampire.

But I wouldn't mind her sexy mouth on my neck.

Her phone rings, and I can't think of a better time to escape. She's still scratching Chance's belly, though, so we're not going anywhere.

She digs through her purse for her phone. "Where is the damn thing," she growls. Finally, she pulls it out and answers. "Hey, Daisy."

Daisy? My ears perk up almost as much as Chance's do. On second thought, I think I'll stay for another minute. I inch a little closer to eavesdrop. I haven't met many women named Daisy in my lifetime, though there are probably hundreds in the city. She leans down to Chance again, and the top of her dress gaps just enough to give me a perfect view of her large breasts. *Look away.*

"I'm in Central Park. I was just attacked by the sweetest three-legged dog." She laughs, then stands up and steps away from us. "No, I'm fine. He just licked me like a lollipop, stuck his paw down my dress, and now I'm rubbing his belly. So what's up?"

I'm amazed at how Chance is responding to this beautiful woman with the snarky mouth. He usually growls or retreats when a stranger comes near. He's as attracted to her as I am. What is it about her that draws us in?

She licks her lips.

I wonder what she tastes like. Maybe sweet like peaches and cream or spicy like cinnamon. *What the fuck am I thinking?* Who cares what she tastes like? Maybe chocolate-covered strawberries. If she tastes like vanilla, I'm a goner. I lick my own lips with delight. *Get a fucking grip!*

Maybe it's her light-colored eyes or her lack of makeup... maybe it's her full lips. Does her skin tingle as my eyes trace along her long, toned legs? I let my gaze travel lower until I notice the toe ring she's wearing. My pulse surges. A toe ring? Why in the world would I find that so attractive? I squeeze my eyes shut and turn away. Dehydration! Yep, that's my problem. I forgot my water bottle when I left the penthouse.

No, it's called a dry spell.

I tug on Chance's leash again, and he finally rolls to his side and stands up. He does one of those head-to-tail dogquakes, shaking the grass and dirt off his fur. She glances our way and holds up a finger for us to wait. Why should I wait? And why hasn't she walked away? I know I'm being an asshole. Wait. If I'm an asshole, then why am I still standing here?

Now I'm plain confused. I just wanted to go for a run. She continues to talk and I continue to listen.

"Daisy, everything's ready for the opening on Friday. I put most of the photographs where you instructed but switched a couple around."

She drapes her thick, wavy dark hair over one shoulder, revealing her bare, kissable neck. I wish I had my camera. I'd take a thousand pictures of her beautiful curves. They'd never be seen by the public eye—just mine.

"I know you said he's adamant about the order of the photographs, but trust me, they work better where I've hung them." *This is too weird.* "Just stop by tomorrow, and I'll prove it. It's not like he'll be there for the opening anyway." *Huh?* "He'll never know."

Her fingers massage her eyebrows. "I've been doing this for a long time. Just wait until you see it tomorrow. Come any time after nine." She pauses to listen. "Okay. See you then."

No matter how much I want to leave, I can't keep my eyes off this addictive woman or stop listening to her voice. Why does it feel like my life has taken a dramatic left turn by meeting her? This Daisy friend of hers better not be who I think she is.

My agent and my sister.

I press the button for the twentieth floor and step to the back of the elevator. Chance sits patiently beside me. The elevator door is about halfway closed when a hand with long dark fingernails stops it. My neighbor, Candy, walks in, twirling a lollipop in her mouth.

Don't think of licking the woman in the park. Don't think it! Too late.

"Hi, Julius," she purrs.

"Hi, Candy," I say dryly.

Eyes locked on my face, she pulls the lollipop slowly

out of her plastic mouth. *Pop*. "Funny meeting you here. You're exactly the person I was hoping to see today. I tried knocking on your door, but no one was there." She pouts. "Something seems to be wrong with my bedroom ceiling fan. It's so hot, and the AC isn't working well. I don't like sleeping naked unless someone's in the bed with me. Could you come over later and look at it?" She flutters her fake eyelashes, and one springs loose at the side of her right eye. She doesn't seem to notice, because she keeps fluttering.

I focus my attention on the elevator panel. The tenth-floor button flashes. *Why is this elevator so damn slow?*

"I'm not available. Ask maintenance to check it out."

"Oh, poo. Why don't you come over for a drink instead? Bring Chancy Wancy with you." She bends over to pet him, but he bares his teeth and growls. She yanks her hand back. "He's so sweet."

Every time I see this woman, something somewhere in her place is broken and she wants me to fix it. Or she asks if I could move a heavy piece of furniture. She's recently divorced and, according to Daisy, is now worth several million dollars. She could call anyone to handle these problems, but she asks me—the worst person in the world. And I say no, so then comes the invite to have a drink. I don't answer her about that because she already knows my response. She's persistent, I can tell you that.

Ding. Finally!

I motion for her to go out first and then follow behind. That's about the nicest I get. *Five, four, three, two, one...*

Right on cue, she stops at her door, turns, and leans back against it. "Well, in case you decide to stop by, I'll make sure I've got some cold beers in the fridge for you." She rubs the lollipop up and down her tongue and her loose eyelash waves goodbye.

I get my door unlocked and open as quickly as possible. Chance doesn't waste a minute dragging me inside, as anxious to escape her as I am. I'm done. The woman at the park is about all I can handle today. I toss my keys on the table near the door and unhook Chance's broken leash. He trots over to his water dish.

I walk through the living room toward the kitchen. "Daisy? Are you home?" I grab a bottle of water from the fridge, then toss the leash in the garbage. I pull out a stool at the kitchen island and begin sifting through a small stack of mail.

Chance ambles toward me with his favorite ball in his mouth, then flops down next to my stool. No matter where I am, he's never too far away. We don't know his past, but when he arrived at the pound, he was on the brink of death. His leg had to be amputated. The vet believes he was severely abused. It makes my blood boil, because I know what that feels like. I offer him a couple of dog treats from the bowl on the counter.

Daisy and I live together. I bought this penthouse a couple of years ago after our aunt died and my career really kicked off. It's a large open space with three bedrooms. There is enough room for two people, and we each have our own corner if we want to be alone. It works because neither one of us is in a relationship. We have a dark past and no other living relatives, so we stick together.

The best part of this place is that it has a connecting apartment with a separate entrance that I use as my studio. The person who lived here before us ran his business from home. Daisy and I have our own offices and enough room to run my photo shoots. It's an ideal setup.

Daisy walks out of her bedroom. "Here I am," she says happily. She places her exercise sneakers on the floor, then leans against the kitchen counter wearing her favorite running shorts and crop top. "I have a surprise for you. Guess who called today to discuss your work and a possible exhibit?"

I shuffle through a list of possibilities in my head. I say the first two names that come to mind. She shakes her head, excitement sparkling in her eyes. Okay... There is one gallery in the city I've—well, *Daisy* has—been trying for nearly two years to get me into. It couldn't possibly be. I feel a smile spreading across my face.

"Come on. Just say it!" She bounces in place with a gigantic smile.

"No way. Don't tell me that the Mossi Krelo Gallery wants to exhibit my work!"

Her arms shoot up in the air. "Yes! Jacqueline Krelo called this afternoon. They love your black and white bodyscape photography... and your name, of course."

I jump up and give her a big hug. "Thank you so much! I can't believe it. All these years you've been trying, and it was always no."

"Patience is key. You've made a name for yourself,

and it's blowing through the streets of New York City and other major cities. People are talking."

I brace my hands on the countertop and bow my head to contain myself. *I did it. I finally did it.* My dream to be a black and white photographer started when I was in my teens. My mom gave me a camera for my thirteenth birthday, and my ambition exploded from there. So many people in the past had said I'd never be able to accomplish my dreams because of the problems I have. Their doubts pushed me even harder. And look where I am today.

Daisy wraps her arm around my shoulder. "Congrats, Jules. You deserve it, but—"

I drop back onto the stool and cross my arms. "You know how I hate when you say *but*."

"There's only one itsy bitsy condition." She steps back and bites her lip. "You have to attend opening night."

Chance walks over and drops his ball at her feet. Perfect distraction. She bends down and scratches his head. "How are you, my cutie? Want to play fetch?" She picks up the ball. He barks and sits on his haunches. His eyes don't leave her hand. She tosses the toy into the living room, and he scrambles after it.

I drag my hands through my hair. She swats my hand away from my head and I lean away. "Stop doing that to your hair all the time. You're going to go bald."

"Whatever. So what did you say to her?" I don't do public appearances.

"I told her I'd get back to her. If you want this as bad as you say you do, you're just going to have to suck it up. I know details and people are superfluous to you—you just want to sell your photographs. But I wish you'd start to come to the openings. Get to know people. It'll increase your sales."

"Why are we having this conversation again? You know I'm a loner and keep to myself. I'm not a talker."

She leans over the counter and grabs a banana from the fruit bowl. "Oh, I don't know. Maybe because you need to stop hiding behind your work and start interacting with people. With your fans."

"Whatever. Don't talk to me about hiding behind something, Ms. Tattoo."

She flips me the bird, then splits open the banana. "That's a low blow. You can try, but you're not going to turn this conversation to be about me. It's not gonna work."

Daisy is covered from head to toe with light-colored tattoos. They're gorgeous. She started getting them in her late teens—they made her feel better in her skin. Her shoulder-length hair is dyed a silver-blond; well, that's what she told me the color is. I only see gray. She looks like a piece of art herself.

"I interact with people every day on the streets and during photo shoots."

The banana is halfway to her mouth again, but she stops before she takes another bite. "Bull. You blend into crowds so no one sees you. You hardly even speak to your models. You tell them what positions to assume and then when you're done, most of the time, you dismiss them immediately with barely even a thank you. That's not interacting. That's being a dick."

"So? Don't you always say my middle name is Dick? I have a rep to protect," I joke. Her lips purse.

"*Anywayyyyy*, your exhibition at Nouveau Exposures opens this Friday night. It's also the gallery's official opening. It's a great place. The manager, Skylar, is cool, young, and beautiful. She really knows her stuff, and we get along well."

I crack my neck. "You've told me this several times."

"Well, sometimes I wonder if you ever listen to me. Why don't you come to this one as a test run? It's a smaller venue. It'd be a huge hit for you and for the gallery." She takes the last bite of the banana and throws the peel in the garbage.

"People go to galleries for paintings and photographs, not to see the artist."

"That's not true, and you know it. Come on, big brother. Give it a try." She bends over and picks up one of her sneakers.

I know she's right, but I'm not going to budge. How weird would it be if this Skylar she's mentioned is that woman from the park? Again, how many Daisies can there be who are involved with openings. Let me try to find out.

"So Chance plowed over a woman today in Central Park. That new leash you bought was a piece of shit. He bolted after a squirrel and it just snapped in two. It amazes me how fast he can run with only three legs. And since when does he like squirrels? But he knocked her flat on her ass."

"Holy shit. Did she get hurt? We don't need a lawsuit on our hands."

"Give me a break. When she tried to get up, Chance got his paw stuck in her dress and scratched her chest. Just a little one. But she was covered in coffee and dirt, and didn't seem to like me very much."

Daisy snorts. "I wonder why. But Chance running off like that is out of character. Maybe it was just pent-up energy. It's been so hot, we haven't been walking him as much." She finishes tying her sneaker, then picks up the other one.

"Maybe. She must've tasted really good... he wouldn't stop licking her. I was waiting for him to start humping her leg."

She giggles. "That's strange. He usually growls or snaps at strangers. He doesn't lick them." She shrugs her shoulders. "You know how Chance loves anything vanilla like you do. Maybe that's what she tasted like." Is God testing my restraint? But it doesn't matter because I won't see her again.

"How am I supposed to know what she tastes like?" Why am I being defensive and answering a question she didn't ask? She eyes me with suspicion.

"Was she pretty?"

A few seconds of silence fills the air because I don't know how to answer her. It feels like a loaded question, and I usually don't talk about women this way.

"Well, was she or wasn't she?" She removes the hair band from around her wrist and proceeds to put her hair up in a ponytail. "It's not a difficult question."

I rake my hand through my hair again. Daisy shoots me a warning look. "She's beautiful." *More than beautiful.* "Truthfully, she's the first woman I've noticed in a long time. Her curves were perfect. I photograph women all the time, but her—" My pulse races just talking about her. "I don't know. There was something special about her. It doesn't matter, though, because I didn't even get her name. Chance tried to follow her when she left." *So did I.* "She walked away after she told me to have fun being a lonely, miserable bastard for the rest of my life." Daisy chokes on a laugh, then covers her mouth.

"Sorry. I know I shouldn't laugh, but maybe you should dig down deep and think about what a stranger said to you just after meeting you for a few minutes." I press my lips together and my shoulders slouch.

"I deserved it and I felt bad after. I could've handled the situation differently."

A smirk grows on Daisy's face.

"What's that look for? No, ya know what? Forget I asked. I'm not in the mood for a therapy session."

She glances at her watch. "I don't have the time anyway. But really quick. Did you get your new contacts and sunglasses today? How are they?"

"They're even more comfortable than the last ones. The technology keeps getting better and better."

"Glad to hear it. Well, I can't look at our treadmill anymore. I'm going for a run. Think about Friday night. If you don't want to do it for yourself, do it for me. I don't ask for much."

"Fine," I say through gritted teeth. "I'll think about it."

"That's better than nothing." She pulls a water bottle out of the refrigerator. "It sounds like Chance got enough exercise with your beautiful mystery woman. I'll leave him here with you."

"Yeah, I don't think he's interested anyway." I angle my head to the living room. She peeks over my shoulder and laughs. Chance is dead asleep in his bed, belly up, and snoring away. I love that dog.

3

SKYLAR

In a dark, quiet room, I stand frozen in place as the guy from the park circles around me like I'm his prey. Every hard angle of his face is emphasized and his red eyes blaze as they lock with mine. Maybe it should scare me. But it doesn't. It only excites me. He stops behind me and his heat embraces my naked body like a blanket. His fingers lightly brush my hair to one side, revealing my neck. Goosebumps dance along my skin, and I shiver. My arms won't move, as if they are bound behind me. I let my head fall back against his hard chest. Electrifying sensations explode through my body as his needy lips press the skin under my ear, then trail burning kisses down my slender neck and shoulder. My breath comes in pants as I arch my back, pushing my sensitive, swollen breasts forward. When his hands skim from my neck down, my knees weaken. I jolt away from his possessive touch when his fingers trace the mark on my heaving chest. I look down, and the scratch turns into a bleeding heart... a broken heart.

Before I can look at his face, the song "Girl on Fire" blasts in the distance, sucking me out of the darkness. I jolt awake. A sheet is tangled around my waist, I'm horny as hell, and I'm sweating like I've been sitting in a sauna for hours. My damn phone alarm is screaming the same song from my dream. After a few deep breaths, I rid myself of the bedding, and stumble to the bathroom to look in the mirror. The scratch is just as it was when I went to bed, but I can still feel the searing pain from the dream.

I brace myself on the sink and drop my chin to my chest. The guy from the park consumes my dreams. This wasn't the first time. And the dreams get steamier and steamier. Sadly, this is the only action I've had in months. It feels like years. I huff, then grab my toothbrush. *Stop feeling sorry for yourself. It's time for work.*

Two hours later, I'm sitting in my office at the gallery, measuring the performance of a Facebook ad that has been running to promote the Nouveau Exposures grand opening. My eyes sting from staring at the screen. I should've been a lot more productive since I arrived, but that stupid dream is still a major distraction.

I push my chair away from my white desk, stand up, and stretch my arms over my head. My reflection in the mirror on the adjacent wall reveals that my eyes aren't as puffy as they were when I left my apartment this morning. Good.

After I wash my coffee cup and apply some lip gloss, I straighten up my desk. My goal is to be as neat and organized as possible in this office. My apartment is another story. Some days I walk in the door at home and wince. I'm not dirty, I'm just a mess. I won't let that happen here, though.

I stroll into the showroom and give it another once-over. If someone truly looks at any gallery, the space looks pretty boring. Plain white walls and shiny hardwood floors. But it's meant to be that way. It's a clean backdrop for the paintings or photographs that will be hung on them one day. They are the decorations. And boy, do I love the photographs hanging on the walls in this place. I can't wait for the opening.

Daisy Levi should arrive any minute. Every photograph is in its perfect place. I've posted prices and titles on the walls next to the corresponding works, as requested. The photographer, Julius Ariti, is pretty particular—he wants everything displayed his way. Well, if he wants them *his* way, he should show up Friday night. I've made a few changes, and I'm hoping that Daisy, Julius's agent, will agree to how I've arranged them now. I'm pushing my luck, but it's worth the try.

I'm kind of obsessed with researching last names and their meanings. I've admired Julius Ariti for years, and when we landed him for the gallery opening, I had to look into his name. It sounds noble—Julius Ariti. Maybe Greek or Italian. I found out it's of Greek origin, but I had to laugh when I learned that it means friendly, generous, and approachable. Everything I've read and heard about him sounds like the complete opposite. More like a cactus.

He's one of the most famous black and white photographers in the United States, and he's only thirty-three. Rumor has it that he's hard to work with, antisocial, and a bit high on himself, which is disappointing. It'd be a dream to meet him, but from what his agent says, that won't happen. He doesn't attend his exhibits. Instead, Daisy handles everything and attends the openings for him. She's a tough businesswoman. She's a little intimidating, too, with her body full of tattoos. But once I got to know her, she's pretty cool and easygoing.

I recently moved here from Boston to open and manage the Nouveau Exposures Gallery. We specialize in black and white photo-based exhibits. Monica Morrison, the owner, arrives tomorrow. She also owns the gallery I worked at in Boston. She used her long line of connections to get an exhibit by the one and only Julius Ariti for our opening. It wasn't easy, but she won. It's such an honor to have his photographs displayed here.

I've been surrounded with art since I was born. My mother is an artist. I didn't inherit any of her creative genes, but I love anything that revolves around art and photography. As long as I don't have to create anything myself.

My last name is Vitale. It's Italian in origin, but comes from the Latin word vita, meaning *life*. I'd say I'm full of life—well, that's if I've had my daily dose of caffeine. Most people know to avoid me if I haven't.

That guy and his dog at the park yesterday were lucky I didn't lose my shit when I dropped my coffee. No one gets between me and my caffeine kick.

Light taps on the entrance door grab my attention. Daisy smiles and waves through the glass. I unlock and open the door. "Hey, Daisy." She traipses in, plonks a box on the black front desk by the door, then turns toward me. We air kiss. "How are you today?" I ask. "Double espresso like always?"

She shakes her head and plops into a visitor's chair in front of the desk, fanning herself. "I'm too hot. Give me a few minutes. So much for the humidity going away. I thought the rain the other night was supposed to help. It's only nine, and I'm already zapped of energy. It feels damn good in here. I need a weekend away in the Hamptons or somewhere away from this sticky city."

"Just say the word, darlin'!" I sit across from her at the desk and push the box to the side. "My sister moved there a couple months ago. She can hook us up with something."

Lacey Devlin is my stepsister, and she just moved out to the Hamptons to live with her boyfriend, Will. We met Will and his twin brother, Josh, when we took a vacation to St. Thomas in April. They fell fast and hard for each other. What they thought would be just a hot fling has turned into happily-ever-after. Will and Josh own a marina, and Lacey now works with them.

"Is that whose apartment you moved into?" Daisy asks.

I nod with a smile. Lacey and I lived together when I first moved here. It sucks that she moved, but now I have her great apartment.

"Will she be here Friday?"

"No." I sigh. "But she'll be in the city on Sunday with her boyfriend. They plan on stopping by to see the gallery then."

"Too bad they'll miss the opening. But back to the Hamptons." She grins. "I'd be totally up for a girls' weekend. I need a good dose of fresh air and some sand between my toes."

I point to her arm. "Are your tattoos sensitive in the sun?"

Daisy is tall, thin, and a piece of art herself. Her tattoo artist is brilliant. Tattoos do nothing for me, especially on women, but they work for her. They're… feminine. All pastel colors and soft edges. They compliment her gorgeous silver-blond hair and magnificent blue eyes. She knows how to dress too. Her slate blue halter-top jumpsuit looks impeccable. It's the perfect color for both her eyes and her tattoos.

"Not really. I just have to use a lot of sunscreen. No different from anybody else." Suddenly, her eyes bulge and she leans forward. "What the hell happened to your chest, girl? And how didn't I see that when I came through the door? Does it hurt?"

I look down. The scratch on my chest is redder now than it was when I woke up this morning.

"Ugh. This is what I got for going to Central Park yesterday. All I wanted was to enjoy my iced coffee and the fresh air, but no. I told you I'd just been run over by a dog when you called. I had a cute strapless minidress on. The dog's damn paw got caught in the top of the dress somehow, and my boobs almost flashed everyone around us." Daisy bursts out laughing, but then she zones in on the scratch again. Her smile disappears and her eyebrows crinkle.

"I'm pissed because opening night is in two days, and I planned on wearing a strapless dress. It better not get infected. I doused it with an antiseptic when I got home last night and before I came to work."

"Don't worry. Remind me on Friday—I have some great makeup that'll fix you right up." She snags a tissue from a box on the desk and blots her nose and forehead with it. "Don't dogs have to be on a leash?"

"Supposedly it broke when the dog took off after a squirrel. Of course, he landed on me instead. His name was Chance. He only had three legs, but he ran like he was the bionic dog. Two different colored eyes. Freaking adorable!" Did she just jump when I said *Chance*, or am I imagining things?

Her crossed leg begins to wag, and she rubs the back of her neck. "Did you see the owner? Did he apologize?"

"How did you know the owner was a he?"

Eyes wide, she waves her hand at me. "He… she… whoever." She shifts in her seat and starts swinging her leg. I shrug.

"The owner was hot with the most amazing reddish-brown eyes. I've never seen eyes that color before. Once he opened his mouth, his sex appeal disappeared. Well, maybe just a little. He was cold, but every once in a while his face softened, like it was an act and he had a rep to protect." Her leg swings faster.

Why can't she sit still all of a sudden? Maybe she has to use the bathroom. "Are you okay?"

She stops her leg with her hand. "Yeah… Why?"

"You seem antsy all of a sudden. Oh, never mind. It was weird, though. He kept looking at me all squinty, then he put his sunglasses on. Anyway, guys are idiots."

"And that's why I avoid men." Daisy laughs and I join in.

"Me too."

Normally, I wouldn't talk to an agent like this, especially in a business environment, but Daisy's cool and we hit it off like we're old friends. I finally have someone here to talk about art with who's around my age and won't fall asleep from boredom. Speaking of art…

"Anyway, tell me. What can I do to convince the renowned Julius Ariti to attend the opening? There has to be something. It'd be even better publicity for us." I wave my hands in the air. "The brand-new gallery that was blessed with his presence. The reporters attending would love it."

She shakes her head regretfully. "Absolutely nothing. I can't even convince him. He's very private. He doesn't attend openings, no matter what he's offered. I do what he tells me to because he pays me to do it. And believe me, it's not easy at times. On that note, let's see what you've done with the photographs." She stands up and begins inspecting the displays. "Hmm. You changed photographs one and two for fourteen and fifteen."

My stomach twists, but I stand tall to show confidence in my decision. "I did. What do you think?"

She clasps her hands behind her neck. "Why?"

"That's easy. With these two, it's amazing that he could capture the curves from elderly women in a way that looks like rolling troughs of The Wave in Arizona. The different textures of their skin create the same ripple effect. Even though the photos are black and white, I can picture their original terracotta and red colors. These are the first pictures visitors will see when they come through the door. They're visible from the street and will hopefully draw pedestrians through the door. They're my favorites, and I find they stick out more than the rest. In my opinion, these two are the best photos he's ever taken."

"I'm not sure I'll tell him how much you admire his work. No need to feed his already large ego." She winks at me. "My lips are sealed about the switch. You're brave—no one has ever challenged his requests. But I like that about you. You challenge him, and you've never met him."

Maybe it'd be better not to meet him. I know I have him on a pedestal. I'd hate to be disappointed. I know what the rumors are, but I'll keep my impression until I'm proven wrong.

Daisy laughs. "You do that."

"What? Did I say that out loud?" She chuckles again. My cheeks start to burn. I need to save myself. *Coffee.* I'll offer her some coffee. "How about an espresso now?"

"Sure. I'd love my usual double. I can't stay too much longer, though. I have another appointment." We walk back to the front desk and she sits down.

"Okay. I'll be right back." As the espresso brews in my office, my thoughts wander. I can't help but be jealous of all the women he photographs. So many of his photos are of beautiful, naked female bodies. It's not like I want to be one of them. At least I'm trying to convince myself of that.

"So. Back to Julius," I say as I walk toward Daisy,

and then almost spill the cup when a dog barks frantically on the street. "What the hell?" The barking halts for a second then starts up again, but it's farther away. I place her cup in front of her, then walk over to the window.

"Did you hear that? I didn't think I'd be jumpy about a dog. It sounded like it was right outside the door, but I don't see one."

"I heard a dog, but it didn't seem so unusual." I walk back to her and sit down. She takes a careful sip of the espresso. "Mmm, that's good. You're really curious, aren't you? More than most."

"About what? The barking dog?"

She shakes her head, then places the cup back on the saucer. "No. Julius."

"Oh. Yes. Every picture I've ever seen of him on the internet or in interviews, they're only a silhouette. He's so mysterious. What's he hiding? I'd love to pick his brain, find out why he is the way he is, how he became a photographer, why he only takes black and white photos. I know some of that information is out there, but I'd love to get up close and personal. Can't you just introduce me as your friend?"

"I know you're fishing, but I can't reveal a thing. Privacy and data protection. You know the drill."

"I know. I know. It's just that I love his work, and I've been following him for years. Having his work in this gallery is a dream come true. If I could, I'd buy every piece we've got on display here. Ugh! Listen to me! Okay, I'll stop now. It's probably better that he doesn't come. I don't need the pressure or the disappointment if he's not who I expected."

Daisy pats the side of the box she brought with her. "Back to work. Do you have scissors handy?"

I take a pair out of a drawer and hand them to her.

"Thanks. Here are the pamphlets to put on display during his exhibit. They list all the photographs you have displayed here as well as others that are available for purchase."

"I think we're going to have a full house on Friday. Almost every invitation we sent out has been accepted." I pull a sheet of paper out of a folder. "Here's the list of those who've said yes."

"Good, thanks. Hopefully, some of them will be ready to buy."

"I'm confident it will go well." *I hope, anyway.* "I've been working social media like crazy. I've had a great response. We've had lots of page views on the website, and I've sent out a couple of newsletters. Plus the ads in the newspaper. I really think we're in a good place." *And don't forget the free champagne.*

Outside, I look like I have everything under control. And I do, but my insides are in knots. This is the first opening I've been in charge of. I've been heavily involved with other ones but never the queen bee. Monica has been guiding me, but she's given me free rein with this one since she's in Boston. This is my chance to shine.

There'd better not be any unexpected surprises.

4

JULIUS

The woman from yesterday has consumed every ounce of me. No female has ever gotten inside my head just by looking at her. I got up at five this morning because I was tired of seeing her in my dreams. Even work hasn't been able to hold my attention today.

After we parted ways, Chance tried with all his strength to follow her but what was left of the leash held that time. I found myself disappointed, and it confused the shit out of me. He whined until she was out of sight.

But still, she was on the phone with a girl named Daisy. When I told Daisy what happened, she didn't act like she knew anything... except I heard the woman mention something about pictures and that she'd meet Daisy at nine this morning.

And Daisy went out early today specifically to stop by the gallery.

What are the chances?

So that's why I'm here, standing at the corner near the gallery as if I'm undercover. I need to see if it's the same woman. If it is, her name is Skylar. The name fits her. And what should I do if it is her? Walk in and introduce myself officially as Julius Ariti, dick extraordinaire? Or should I tell her my real name, Julius Levi? Why do I even care?

Chance looks up at me and whines. Okay. Time to get this over with. It's probably not her anyway, and I can put all this stupid shit behind me and go hide in my studio… like the miserable bastard I am.

Maybe I don't want to be miserable anymore.

"Come on, buddy. We need to make this quick." Chance walks ahead of me, his nose held high, smelling everything in sight. I tug on the leash as we get closer to the gallery. If it is her, I don't want her or Daisy to see me. I bend down to pick up Chance, and he licks my cheek several times. To quote the maybe Skylar, *this is fucking ridiculous*. A couple more steps, and I'm at the edge of the gallery window.

There's Daisy, sitting alone at a desk facing away from the window. Good. And then another woman comes into view, approaching Daisy with a cup in hand. Probably an espresso—Daisy drinks that stuff like water. As long as it's not alcohol, I don't care what she drinks.

Suddenly, Chance starts barking and struggling to get out of my arms. Shit! It *is* the woman from yesterday. My stomach clenches and my pulse pounds in my ears. He recognizes her too. I retreat quickly, feeling excited, not disappointed. Now what do I do?

I start walking. Aimlessly. I should be in my fucking studio, working on my next project. Focusing only on work. Not sweating my ass off out here, trying to come to terms with what's bugging me. Skylar is my problem. I don't have time for her.

Daisy, Chance, and my career are my only priorities. There's no room for anyone else. Not even this beautiful stranger who put me in my place yesterday. Why is she so special?

Honestly, it's killing me that I can't see her the way she truly is.

The way most people see her.

In color.

"Chill out. I'm coming."

It's about time. After knocking on this door three times already, I was about to give up. The door swings open, and Cameron stands there in pink boxer shorts. It's one in the afternoon.

"Julius?" He looks over his shoulder, then down at his half-naked body. "Th–This is a surprise." He moves to the side and motions for me to come in.

"Do you always answer your door in boxers? Your doorbell doesn't work, by the way."

"I know. If I knew you were coming, I would've at least put on a shirt."

Cameron is going for his master's in photography and assists me sometimes when I need an extra person for one of my shoots. He also runs special errands for me once in a while when I'm in a bind.

I step inside, and it's all I can do to keep from cringing. Not so much because of what I'm seeing, but because of what it reminds me of. Memories of my past flash before my eyes, almost knocking me over. With a deep breath, I move forward and push the past back in its black box where it belongs.

His small studio apartment looks like it hasn't been cleaned or renovated in years. The condition of the building when I walked in should've alerted me to that, but for some reason I'm surprised. The kitchen is about the size of my walk-in closet. A battered table and two chairs stand in the middle. The appliances look like they're older than I am. The chipped sink is filled with dishes. The linoleum is faded and cracked.

The back of my neck feels itchy because my thoughts want to travel somewhere else. Somewhere I don't want to go. *Find something to focus on.*

Cameron clears his throat. "Is everything okay? Can I get you something to drink?"

My muscles jerk a little bit. "Why wouldn't I be okay?"

He props his hand on his hip. "Julius, you've *never* been to my apartment. I didn't even think you knew where I lived. I would've cleaned if I knew you were coming."

"Well, now you know." My eyes scan the cramped living space again. "How long have you been living here?"

"Since I started graduate school. Look, I know this place is a dump, but it's all I can afford. I want to live in the city, so it's just something I have to deal with."

I shove my hands in my pockets. "I guess."

Cameron has been working for me for over a year,

and I never knew that he was living in a place that looks like it could fall apart at any moment. *Because you only think about yourself.* When he shows up for work, he always looks like he came straight from the dry cleaner—crisp button-down shirt with pressed slacks. His black shoes look like he polishes them every day. Looks can be deceiving.

This place reminds me of my childhood, and it doesn't feel good. The biggest difference is that he doesn't seem to care. I cared, but it wasn't my choice. I was a kid. It's hard to believe someone with ambitions like Cameron has, has to live like this. Actually, no one should have to.

There's a pile of clothes on a chair in the corner. He walks over, grabs a pair of jeans off the top, and proceeds to put them on. "So what's up? I have class in an hour."

"Do you have plans tomorrow night?"

"Nothing major. Just hangin' with my boyfriend. Why?"

"Can you watch Chance for me again? It'd only be a couple hours. I have somewhere to go, and Daisy will be at that opening for my bodyscape collection. You can hang out at my place and order in. My treat."

He cocks an eyebrow skeptically. "Can my boyfriend come with me? I know how private you are, but—"

"He touches my shit, you die."

His eyes widen.

"Cameron, lighten up. I'm just kidding."

"I'm the one who should lighten up?" He points his thumb at his chest. "Are you sure you're okay? Do you have a fever? You… You're different today. I guess I don't see you outside of work much, but… And why didn't you just call me? Why the hell did you come all the way over here?"

"What's with all the questions?" My voice is harsher than I meant it to be. Cameron's face deflates. Truth is, I don't know the answers. I just know I feel like a different person than I was yesterday.

"Sorry. I'm just surprised you came here. Forget it."

"Okay. So you'll come?" My voice is a little friendlier this time.

"Yeah, sure. What time?"

"Does six thirty work for you?"

"Shouldn't be a problem. I'll let you know if something changes."

"Great. Don't say anything to Daisy, though. She'll be busy with the opening."

His eyebrow tweaks upward, and I can tell he wants to ask more questions. *Time to escape.*

"Thanks for your help." I reach out my hand. Now both of his eyebrows touch his hairline. *What the hell?* He glances at my hand, then slowly wraps his around mine. I shake it firmly, then let go. "See you tomorrow night."

Once I'm out of the building, I take a deep breath. Daisy and I grew up in a place like this. Only our place wasn't just decrepit or old. It was dirty, dangerous, and deadly. I look back at it and wonder where we'd be right now if Aunt Marie hadn't taken us into her Brooklyn home when we were in high school. I don't think I'd be a successful photographer. And Daisy or I might've ended up like Mom or our father. It gives me the chills just thinking about it.

Aunt Marie was a saint for taking in two fucked-up kids the way she did. She knew it wouldn't be easy, but she refused to let us be separated and sent to different foster homes. Once she died, I kind of closed off again. I let my work become even more of an obsession, and I kept everyone at a distance. I felt safer and less vulnerable that way.

But what I plan on doing tomorrow will rip my world wide open.

5

SKYLAR

"Look! It's gone!" Daisy turns me around to face the mirror in the bathroom. She clasps her hands to her chest and leans in, waiting for my response.

I twist back and forth. "Either you're awesome or the makeup is. One less thing to worry about. I don't know which was worse, my blotchy chest from my nerves or the scratch from the dog. Anyway, you fixed it!" I use my hand to fan the air in front of my face. The AC is running full blast and I've got my hair up in a classy bun to help me stay cool, but it's not working. I'm sweating like hell.

"I know this is a big night for you, Skylar, but you need to bring your nerves down a notch," she says, placing her makeup in her makeup case.

"It's a *huge* night for me." This opening could make or break my career. If tonight isn't a success, Monica could easily decide I'm not the one for this job.

"You're right," Daisy says. "It is huge. But the gallery looks awesome. Everything's ready to go, and we still have time before the door opens." We head over to my office. I take a deep breath and then blow it out.

"I can't thank you enough for all your help and encouragement. You'd think you worked here. You've gone way out of your way, more than any agent I've ever met."

She leans in close and whispers, "You're one of the youngest I've worked with, not as annoying, and you're just plain cool."

"What's all the whispering about?" Monica joins us, holding three flutes and a champagne bottle in her hands.

"Look, Daisy made that scratch magically disappear."

She places the glasses and bottle on the desk. "Even more reason to celebrate. Let's have a little sip before we open the door."

Daisy raises her hand. "Sorry. Nothing for me. I don't drink." *Oops*. "But thanks anyway. Give me a second, and I'll get some sparkling water instead. No toasting without me."

"She's so down-to-earth. With the reputation Mr. Ariti has and all those tattoos… she looks like a tough cookie, but she's really a sweetheart, isn't she?" Monica pours some bubbly for the two of us.

"She is tough, but if we disagreed on anything, she always met me in the middle. Though that didn't happen much. I'll be sorry to see her go once the exhibit is over. She's been a blessing."

"You didn't need any extra blessings. I've had every confidence in you from the beginning. We've worked together for a long time and you're like a daughter to me. You have quite a future ahead of you, Sky. And you're only twenty-eight. Not many people have the knowledge and experience that you do at your age. You should be very proud of yourself."

I wrap my arms around her. "You have no idea how great that was to hear. Thank you so much for always encouraging and supporting me."

"Here I am!" Daisy pops back into the room. "Time's ticking." We toast to the evening and hope for the best. I excuse myself to go to the bathroom one last time, mostly just to give myself another pep talk before the test of my life begins.

When I enter the showroom again, I give everything one last critical look. Nervous energy is building, so I have to keep myself busy. I adjust a couple of the leather benches, even though they were fine like they were. I turn the beautiful floral arrangement on the bar to face in a different direction. It has white flowers and a little bit of green—not enough that it'll take the attention away from the photographs. A matching arrangement sits pretty on the desk near the entrance.

"It's time," Monica announces, clapping her hands.

I pretend to fix my hair, then smooth down my strapless black taffeta dress that rests just above the knee. Jocelyn lent it to me from the large collection she has at her house. It's classy but still has a smart business flair. Speaking of Jocelyn, she's the first one to walk through the door. Following her is Christian, Sophia, and Drew.

"We're so excited for you. You look beautiful. And that dress is perfect!" Jocelyn gives me a quick hug. "I know there's a line behind us, so I'll make this quick. Good luck, and we'll talk to you later."

I hug them all. "Thank you so much for coming. Now go drink some champagne before it runs out, and have fun."

The next hour flies by, and people come and go. Just like I predicted, *The Wave* sold first. *Take that, Mr. Ariti. Maybe you could learn something from me.* I've spent the hour answering questions and trying to politely influence customers to buy the photographs. The crowd thins slightly, and I sip on a glass of water near the bar.

Monica comes by. "Skylar, can you please help the customer by photograph fifteen? I have to go in the back for a moment."

"Sure." I take a deep breath and leave the bar.

After several questions from the customer and a lot of convincing from me, the man finally caves and says yes. That was a tough one. I lead him to the front where Monica is handling the business end of things.

"Thank you, Mr. Stewart," I say. "Monica will process your purchase. I'm confident *Curves* will look lovely in your office. Have a great evening." We shake hands. Once the transaction is complete, I walk back and put a sold sticker next to the photograph.

"Impressive and convincing. You've done your homework. I would've bought it myself." My stomach twirls like an ice skater performing a sit spin. *It can't be him. Nah.* It's just a man with a similarly chilling yet sexy voice. Why would I even remember his voice? I'm not going to let him ruin this night. *Don't let him see your excitement either… if it is him.* I turn around slowly.

It's him. Here in my gallery. He's mouthwatering in a black button-down business shirt that's cuffed at the elbows and black business pants that he fills out perfectly. He sure does like black and white things.

How and why is he here? Of all the places in a city with a population in the millions, he picks this gallery to come to. And on the most important night of my life.

We stand there eyeing each other, waiting to see who will speak first. His tight jaw ticks, but his eyes are warmer this time. His gaze caresses my body, and I'm reminded of the recurring dreams I've been having. My skin sizzles with heat and I squeeze my legs together.

"You look beautiful tonight," he says. "Then again, you looked beautiful the other day too. Coffee, dirt and all."

"Thank you?" I'm hesitant because I don't know if he's being sarcastic or actually paying me a compliment. Why would he be nice now and not the other day? Maybe he had a bad day. We all have them.

"You're welcome," he responds smoothly.

Sophia and Jocelyn appear behind him, waving at themselves like they're hot. Jocelyn gives me a thumbs-up. This is not a pick-up joint. I ignore them and focus on his face.

"Why— How are you here? You're the last person I expected to see tonight. Interesting coincidence."

He looks around. "Oh. It's no coincidence. I have an interest in black and white photography and I was invited, just like the rest of these people."

"By whom, may I ask?"

"You." He takes a few steps back. "Nice to see that

The Wave sold so quickly. Interesting idea to switch its place with *Curves*." And on that last word, he smirks, turns around, and walks away with his hands in his pockets. My mouth opens and closes like a fish. I follow him from a distance and then stop.

What in the ever-loving fuck? My thoughts scramble. My temples pound. *Think, think!* Did I invite him after I wanted to kill him the other day? I wouldn't forget something like that. How does he know about the change in order of the photos? Where is Daisy? I scan the area for Daisy's hair or tattoos. *Damn*, she's talking to him now. Maybe she invited him. I don't like how close they're standing. Am I jealous?

He glances my way, but he's still listening to whatever Daisy is saying. I shouldn't stare because then I look like I like him, but my feet don't seem to want to move. I haven't been attracted to someone like this in a long time, and I almost want to claim that he's mine.

"Who was that yummy specimen?" Sophia startles me from behind, then comes to stand at my side. Jocelyn stands on the other.

"I don't know. Well, I do, but not." I pinch the bridge of my nose.

"Well, that sounds complicated," Jocelyn comments slyly. "Don't you love complicated relationships? It makes things so much more interesting."

"Relationship? I don't even know his name." My voice rises, and I slap my hand over my mouth. I jut my chin to the side for them to follow me. We huddle in a quiet corner, with me keeping one of my eyes on the lookout for him or if someone needs help. "I met him a couple of days ago." Then I tell them the story, but it's cut short because Daisy is discreetly waving me over. Her face is flushed and tight.

"And now he's here," Sophia says. "It's too bad he sounds like a jerk. Still, he's quite handsome." I nod in agreement.

"I guess I'll have to talk to him again before he leaves." Daisy keeps eyeing me. "Listen, ladies, I'm being summoned. I'll talk to you later."

"Fine," Jocelyn responds. "But we want the full story later."

"No details left out," Sophia adds.

"Whatever," I mumble, then notice Daisy approaching me with a tight lip. My insides twist, but this time it's not for pleasure. Something's wrong.

"What's the matter?" I mutter when she reaches my side. "Is a photograph damaged?"

She shakes her head. "Can we talk for a minute? In your office?"

"Should I be concerned? You're making me nervous."

"Let's see once you hear what I have to say. It'll only take a few minutes." She motions to my office.

"Should we get Monica too?"

"Not yet. I want to talk to you first." She hurries off.

What the fuck could be wrong? The night's been running like clockwork. I go through every possible scenario from all of my past experiences. What could I have missed?

Nobody needs help and everything looks under control. It seems to be slowing down too. I mention to

Monica that I'll be in my office for a minute. Once I'm in there, I grab a red rubber band out of my stash. Back and forth, I pace the floor. *Pull, release. Pull, release.* Some people use stress balls—I pull on rubber bands.

"Skylar," Daisy says from the doorway. I plaster a fake smile on my face like I'm not worried at all. Everything is glorious. I give one more vicious tug on the rubber band, then turn around. Daisy's there, but he's right behind her, the one I just talked to. My jaw drops and my arm twitches. The rubber band shoots from my fingers and zaps him on the neck.

It has to have hurt because that was a tight and thick one.

I move forward. "Sorry." It's the same dry tone he used the other day when he apologized to me. His eyes bulge, then he rubs his neck. When his hand drops, it looks like he has a hickey. *Oops.* I wish I gave it to him. *Focus!*

"Thanks for the warm welcome." He smirks as he removes the rubber band from his shirt. "I think this is yours." He extends his arm and drops it onto my opened hand. I toss it back onto the pile on my desk. Is he trying to be charming?

Daisy clears her throat before I can respond. "Skylar, I'd like to introduce you to someone. From what he says, you've met before." There's an uneasy twang in her voice, and she fiddles with her dress. If she's nervous, who the hell could this guy be?

Then it hits me.

No. No. No. Or maybe… *Yes. Yes. Yes.*

6

JULIUS

Why am I doing this? That's been my favorite and most confusing question ever since I met her. Skylar... The one who's running this gallery and who I can't stop thinking about. I'm standing exactly where I was yesterday when I was spying on Daisy, sweating like hell, and now I feel like I'm going to puke.

Daisy is going to flip when she sees me here tonight. She'll want to know why I didn't tell her, and she'll tell me how unprofessional it is that I just showed up. She might even tell me to leave without telling anyone who I am. But that won't work because once I see Skylar, I won't be able to leave unless someone kicks me out.

I almost called Cameron and told him he didn't need to watch Chance. But I couldn't get myself to do it. I've decided to look at this as a business decision. If I have to attend the opening at Mossi Krelo Gallery, attending this one tonight will give me an idea of what I'll be dealing with. Just as Daisy suggested. Openings aren't new to me. I've been to many, just not my own.

Of course, deep down inside, I know I'm here for Skylar, not work. That scares the shit out of me. Only family comes before my work.

Maybe I'll just pretend I'm a normal person who wants to look at the exhibit. Daisy can play along. But this isn't a joke and Daisy would never do that. I'd be screwing around with my profession and Skylar's. No one would win.

But I've hidden my identity for so long. Do I really want to expose myself like this now? For her?

It's crazy, but the answer is yes.

I hope I don't regret it. I've kept our secrets buried for years. No one needs to know what a fucked-up past Daisy and I have. I also hate pity.

The line is gone outside the entrance, but the gallery is full. As I open the door, a woman welcomes me and hands me the pamphlet Daisy made for this event. I scan the layout of the showroom and notice right away that the photographs are out of order. Daisy knows to instruct the manager to hang the photographs in the exact order I request. But then I see that *The Wave* has already sold, and I bite back my anger.

Where are the pictures that have been moved? Following the layout of the gallery along the freshly polished wooden floors, I check where each one hangs. Daisy seems to be nowhere around, which I'm happy about. It's time to blend in for a little while and try to cool off. Then I skid to a stop, possibly scuffing the floor. Skylar is there, talking to a customer, facing away from me. I don't see her face, but I hear her voice. It's slightly higher in tone than the other day and enthusiastic. Her hair is up in a sexy bun, exposing the shimmering skin that I admired and yearned to touch the other day. My fingertips tingle just thinking about it. I shove my hands in my pockets. The dark dress hugs her hourglass figure, and her strappy heels emphasize her toned calves, leaving few secrets behind.

I inch closer to hear what she's saying. The customer asks good questions, and I know immediately which photograph he's talking about. It's the one that should've been where *The Wave* is. I'm blown away as I listen to how she describes *Curves*, explaining the positions of the models and how they formed rolling hills. It's as if she was in my head when I did the photo session for this specific theme. This is coming from her, not from the information we provide every gallery about each photo. I want to be angry, but everything about her piques my curiosity.

After a few minutes, she finally convinces the man to buy the photo. He was tough to break, but she did it. She walks him to the front, and I watch her graceful moves from afar. She returns and puts a sold sign on it without noticing me.

"Impressive and convincing. You've done your homework. I would've bought it myself." Her back stiffens, then she turns around. Silence follows. "You look beautiful tonight. Then again, you looked beautiful the other day too. Coffee, dirt and all."

"Thank you." She seems leery with her delayed response, and there's no sign of getting a warm welcome.

"You're welcome."

"Why—" Her eyes focus on something behind me, and then suddenly freeze on mine. "How are you here? You're the last person I expected to see tonight. Interesting coincidence."

I look around. "Oh. It's no coincidence. I have an interest in black and white photography, and I was invited just like the rest of these people."

"By whom, may I ask?" She rests her hands on her perfect hips.

"You." Her eyes narrow and I take a few steps back. "Nice to see that *The Wave* sold so quickly. Interesting idea to switch its place with *Curves*." I smirk, then walk away. I don't bother looking back because I know she's watching me.

After I'm out of sight and have a chance to breathe, a cold hand grips my elbow and squeezes. "What the hell are you doing here?" Daisy asks, pulling me into a quiet corner with her back facing the crowd. "Start talking now," she demands through gritted teeth. "You're putting me in a very awkward position. This is so unprofessional. I can't pretend like I don't know you. If you aren't going to divulge who you are, then I want you to leave immediately." *Just like I figured.*

I look over her left shoulder. "I'm—" Daisy almost turns in the direction my eyes are focused. "Don't turn around," I say through tight lips. Skylar stands on the other side of the room next to the bar, and she doesn't hide that she's watching me. Once again her effervescence illuminates the room like she's the reason people are here, not my photographs. Two women walk up to her, then she disappears out of view.

"I don't need to know who you're looking at," Daisy seethes. "It was Skylar in the park, wasn't it? She's the one Chance knocked over."

"How do you know that? Why didn't you say something?"

"I should be asking you that. Are you here because of her? When do you ever think twice about any woman? You are not going to screw up this night for her or yourself just because of your sex drive. Or for me, for that matter. Skylar's become a friend, and I want this opening to be a success for her and you."

"Keep your voice down. I don't want to ruin anything. Since you said I have to attend that other opening, I thought this would give me an idea of what I'd be dealing with. Get my feet wet."

"I call bull. I'm so furious with you right now, but I can't show it." She glances over each shoulder, then back to me. "You *will* stay until closing. I'll introduce you as the photographer, and you *will* let the reporters interview you." She inhales deeply. "You *will* mingle with the crowd too. Now stay here so I can find Skylar. By the way, she doesn't know you're my brother. Let's keep it that way or at least until after closing. Where's Chance?"

"Cameron and his boyfriend are watching him at our place." Her eyebrows rise. I rub my temple. "I know. You don't have to say it. I'm a complete mess."

Daisy shakes her head and walks off. I remain in my spot like an obedient puppy. A few minutes later, she waves me over, then leads me to an office in the back of the gallery.

"Skylar," Daisy calls out as she steps inside.

When I walk through the door, Skylar's jaw drops and her eyes widen. *Ouch!* What the hell just stung my neck? My fingers quickly rub the spot, then I notice a rubber band is stuck to my shirt. Did she shoot a rubber band at me?

"Sorry." She's giving me a taste of my own medicine. I don't like it, but I deserve it. *Maybe you could stop being a dick.*

"Thanks for the warm welcome," I say, removing the band from my shirt. "I think this is yours." I reach out my hand and drop it onto her open palm, deliberately avoiding physical contact.

Daisy clears her throat and fiddles with the collar of her dress. Will Skylar really be that angry when she finds out who I am? "Skylar Vitale, I'd like to introduce you to someone. From what he says, you've met before." She pauses—for effect or out of fear? I don't know. Then she says it.

"This is Julius Ariti."

7

SKYLAR

So much for no unexpected surprises. He probably thinks he's slick with the comments he made about switching the photographs. In a way, I feel like Daisy must be playing a practical joke on me, but no. She's wouldn't do that. I've always wanted to meet *the* Julius Ariti, and here he is—supposedly standing in front of me. But the only person I see is the guy I met in Central Park. And the man in my dreams. My love/hate emotions are themselves fighting for control. How can the guy in the park and this amazing artist be the same person? I take a deep breath, determined to behave in a professional manner.

He extends his hand for me to shake it. I stare at it like it's a foreign object. Why am I afraid to shake it? What if I react to his touch like I did in my dreams? Would it be obvious?

"Skylar?" Daisy says delicately. "I realize this comes as a big shock. I didn't know he was going to make a surprise appearance."

"Well, I wanted this night to be a big hit. I guess it'll be even more now." My voice lacks the enthusiasm the words should have. The thrill I thought I'd have if I met him in person is not here.

I step toward him, reaching out my hand to place it in his. My heart pounds like a rabbit's. Inside, I start to tremble in anticipation of what will happen once our skin touches. Will it be explosive? Will scintillating energy plow through my veins, finding its way to the most sensitive parts of my body? My mouth waters.

"Skylar?" Daisy cuts through the dense air.

I glance at her and then him. Then we all look at my hovering hand. What is wrong with me?

"Daisy and Skylar, are you in here?" Monica calls, her footsteps coming closer to the door. I pull my hand away without touching Julius's. She peeks her head in the office. "Oh. There you are. Sorry to interrupt. I need some help out here."

"Monica, we have a last-minute surprise for you!" My voice overflows with excitement, mostly because I'm happy about the distraction. The focus is now on Julius.

Her face lights up. "Really? What's going on? Is this handsome gentleman buying all the photographs?" She chuckles.

"Wouldn't that be nice?" Julius chimes in.

I motion to him. "This is the one and only Julius Ariti. He's decided to crash the party tonight."

Her cheeks blaze. "Wow. How amazing! It's so great to finally meet you, Mr. Ariti."

"Please, call me Julius." He shakes her hand. Her

face is positively scarlet. I should fan her with a piece of paper.

"I'm—we're big fans of your work. We're honored to have your bodyscaping collection as our first exhibit." Monica continues to shake his hand vigorously with both of hers now. "It's a little late, but can we introduce you to the crowd?"

"Um—" Daisy jumps in.

"Yes. That'd be great." I intercept before either can decline. He shows up with no warning, he's going to do what we say. "I'll make a short introduction. We need to take advantage of him being here."

"Two reporters are still here," Monica adds.

"If I can—" Daisy raises her hand.

"I'll do whatever you'd like. I showed up unexpectedly. It's the least I can do." It's hard to believe this is the same man I met the other day. Something's shady.

Monica's smile grows from ear to ear. Daisy's eyes are the size of saucers. And then there are Julius's amazing eyes, staring only at me. And I'm getting lost in his pools of rich cognac. Boy, could I use one right now. *Damn him!*

"Okay." I clasp my hands together, ensuring I won't be touching him. Something tells me that things will never be the same if I do. "That settles it. Monica, can you please lead Julius to the front? I'll be there in a minute."

"Great. Can the reporters take pictures?" *Probably not.*

Daisy raises her hand again. "That won't be—"

"A problem," Julius interjects.

"Julius," Daisy warns.

"Splendid. Please come with me then. I just can't believe you're in this gallery. You never attend your exhibits, but here you are. What a perfect night!" Monica babbles delightedly as they leave the room. She sees dollar signs.

"Daisy, can you stay here for a second, please?"

She turns in my direction, but doesn't come any closer. "I'm sorry, Skylar."

I walk behind my desk and brace my hands on the edge. "You had no idea he was coming tonight?"

"Zilch." She approaches me cautiously. "Believe me, this isn't how I do business. And it's not how he does it either. I'm just as surprised as you are."

"Did you know he was the one I was talking about from the park?" I sift through the files on my desk to find Julius's biography.

"I had a hunch. How many three-legged dogs with the name Chance run around Central Park every day? He also mentioned your *chance* encounter." She laughs and slaps her hand on the desk. "Get it? *Chance*."

"Haha." I'm not amused. "Did you tell him who I was?"

"No. I don't know how he put two and two together. We didn't have much time to talk."

"Don't get me wrong—I'm ecstatic that he's here. But for someone who's so mysterious and wants to be out of the spotlight, this is a huge deal. I just don't want this to somehow go south because he can't handle the press and attention. That would hurt this gallery's reputation and mine."

"I know. Don't worry about it. It won't happen. I've known Julius forever. Trust me. It'll be fine."

Forever? Are they a couple?

8

JULIUS

I've made my bed, now I have to lie in it.

The reporters are bombarding me with questions, and I'm losing my patience. It's time to end this. They're getting too personal. It's after closing now, anyway, so I no longer have an audience.

Tonight has been a real eye-opener. I haven't socialized this much… ever. I'm surprised I didn't storm out of here a long time ago. It's been a reminder of why I don't do this. But I'd do it again, just to watch Skylar observing me. She's been nearby the whole night, listening to everything I've said.

"Mr. Ariti, one more quick question, please." This reporter, especially, is getting on my nerves. "You never attend any of your openings or exhibits. What made you attend this one?"

I rub the corners of my mouth, wishing I had a glass of water. How do I explain why I'm here if I don't understand it myself? Suddenly, someone's holding out a glass of water in front of me. It's not Daisy's tattooed arm. My eyes trail up the sparkling arm holding the glass, but I already know it's Skylar.

"You looked thirsty," she says with a sweet grin.

"I am. Thanks." When I reach for it, our fingers touch lightly, creating an unexpected sensational spark that makes my hand retreat. In slow motion, we watch the glass fall to the ground and shatter, spewing water everywhere.

Fast-forward an hour later, Daisy and I walk through our door. Chance charges us before we can take our shoes off. I kneel down to greet him. "Hey, buddy. Did Cameron take good care of you? Did you have fun?" He barks and licks my hand, then moves on to Daisy.

Cameron and his boyfriend, Dylan, stand up from the couch. "Hey, Julius. Hi, Daisy. I'm surprised you're home at the same time. How'd the opening go?"

She crosses her arms and taps one foot. "It went better than expected since Mr. Ariti made a special appearance." Cameron's eyes bulge. "We sold more photographs than predicted. The reporters and guests were overjoyed because they got to speak to the one and only."

I turn away and walk to the kitchen. They all follow. Daisy's still mad at me. Our ride home in the taxi was completely silent. I didn't want to talk anyway. I've had enough talking for one night. I know she has every right to be angry, but still, the night was a success, just like she said it would be.

"Wow," Cameron says. "I'm shocked, but that's awesome. I would've loved to have seen their faces when you showed up. And the exhibit—it's one of your best collections so I'm not surprised it sold well. Anyway, we're going to go. We have a party to go to."

I open my wallet and sift through my money. "Here you go. Thanks for watching Chance." I hand him a hundred dollars.

His eyes grow wide. "Julius, I can't take this. It's too much." He tries to hand it back to me, but I ignore him and walk over to the refrigerator. "Come on, man. I can't."

"Listen, I have a bunch of projects I want to start on. I'll need another assistant." I'm scanning the fridge for something to drink. I really want an ice-cold beer, but we don't keep alcohol in the house. "Want to increase your hours and learn more on the job?"

Daisy places two glasses on the counter. "Iced tea?"

I hand her the container and close the door, then focus on Cameron because he has yet to answer me. "Well? What do you say? How many classes are you taking this summer?"

"Only two. I work two days a week at a photography studio."

"Good. So that means your schedule isn't too busy. Are you up for it or not?"

"Hell, I'd quit my job at the studio to work with you as many hours as you'd want."

I chuckle. "Let's not get ahead of ourselves. I'll give you a call in a couple of days, and we can discuss the next steps. Sound good?"

"Thanks, Julius. This means a lot. I won't let you down."

"I know. Now go to your party. Don't drink too much."

He shakes my hand vigorously, then pets Chance. He and Dylan wave to Daisy on their way out the door.

And then the interrogation begins.

"What the hell is going on with you?" The pleasant facade is gone. She's still pissed. "It's like you're a different person. Did aliens come down and suck out your brain and replace it with someone else's?"

I tell her what I saw when I went to Cameron's apartment yesterday and how it didn't sit well with me. "I don't know. I feel bad for the guy. He looks so put together when he comes to work. I didn't expect to see that he lives in a place like we did when we grew up. Ours was worse, though. Aunt Marie took us in and gave us a better life.

"Cameron's a good guy—he works hard. I can give him a chance to make more money while he learns on the job. Professor Johnson was my mentor and helped me get to where I am today. Maybe I can do that for Cameron." I shrug. "Pay it forward."

"Excuse me if I'm a bit stunned. I need to digest this whole evening. Let's go to the living room to continue this conversation. I can't stand in these shoes a minute longer. It's time for my foot massager. That was the best birthday present from you." Daisy kicks off her high heels and carries her drink to the couch.

I follow her and drop to the couch myself. It's been a long day. Chance jumps up and lies across my lap. I drape my arm along his back.

Daisy sets up her electronic massager and gets in

position on her favorite part of the sectional. The vibration of the massager replaces the silence.

"So what's brought on this one-eighty change? You never think about things outside your bubble. You are kind of selfish, you know." She always tells me how it is. No sugarcoating. "First, you're taking Cameron under your wing *and* you showed up at the opening. I know you better than anybody, so I'm sure you understand why I don't get it and am a little hesitant about all these changes." She lets her body relax into the couch and drops her head back.

"I don't know how to explain it. It sounds melodramatic, but meeting Skylar two days ago changed something in me. When she walked away and told me to have fun being a lonely, miserable bastard for the rest of my life, it opened my eyes. You said something similar the same day, and it made me think."

She sits up. "You never told me how you knew Skylar was the same person."

"I overheard her phone conversation with you at the park. She said she'd be at work at nine. Then you said you had to go to the gallery at nine. I… kind of followed you… to see if it was true."

She perks up. "Was that Chance barking? I thought I recognized his bark."

"Yes. He seemed to see her too, or maybe it was you. When I saw her, I suddenly found myself happy. *Happy.* Then I had to think about when the last time was that I felt truly happy. Sure, I have my professional success, but what do I have beside that?"

"You have me and Chance."

"You know what I mean."

She winks at me. I guess she does. We sit quietly for a few minutes, listening to Chance snore and fart. Just when I think she's going to let it go, she starts again.

"It's obvious there's a spark between you and Skylar. What are you going to do about it? You started off on the wrong foot, and that doesn't help business relations. She still doesn't know you're my brother." We never got a chance to talk to her alone because Monica was always there. "The night was over when you dropped that glass." I catch her eye, and we both hold back a laugh.

"That's the second time she can blame me for splashing her with something. The other day, she had coffee. Chance pushed her over, and it went down like a bomb—hit the ground and exploded all over her legs. I'm glad it was an iced coffee. And now the water. Not that water is a big deal, but…"

"We have to talk to her at some point. I really want to apologize… or maybe you should do it. She's so laid back, I'm sure she'll understand. Eventually. Oh, and she's a *major* fan of Julius Ariti, so don't screw it up."

"Big deal. Who am I without the title?"

"Ha. You're the miserable and lonely Julius Levi. Maybe she's the one who'll change all that."

If only it could be that easy.

9

SKYLAR

I unlock the gallery door and swing it open. "I can't believe you're here!" I embrace Lacey and then Will once they walk through the entrance. "Welcome to Nouveau Exposures."

"Wow, Sky. This place is great," Lacey says with amazement. Will takes her backpack and places both of theirs next to the front desk. "We're so damn proud of you. I'm sorry that we kept you waiting." She walks around, then peeks into the back. Will checks out the photos.

"I had plenty to do, so don't worry about it."

"All these pictures are of people, not actual structures?" Will asks, his face close to one of them.

"Yes. Aren't they amazing?" *Dang. Gush much, Skylar?* You'd think I was in love with his photos, not Julius. *What? I need a delete button.*

Lacey moves closer to one. "So the photographer's surrounded by naked people all day? Or is it only women?"

64

"Women of all ages, shapes, and sizes." Now that I know who Julius is, I'm a little jealous that he works with naked women all the time. I tell myself that he probably sees them as subjects, not human beings. And then there's the question of the history between Daisy and Julius.

"I'd love that job," Will jokes. Lacey smacks him in the belly. "*Ooph!*"

"You already see women prancing around in bikinis every day," she protests.

He wraps his arm around her waist and kisses her. "Your body's the only one I want to see dancing around the docks." He pecks her lips, then tickles her. She squeals and pulls away from him.

"You guys are so damn cute, it's sickening. So stop it." I'm joking, but I'm surprised by the surge of jealousy that pumps through me. I want what they have. A guy who loves all of me, not just my body.

I was an early bloomer. It seemed like I woke up one morning when I was fourteen with big boobs and never-ending curves. And that's all guys saw from that point on. They pretend to be in love with me, but all they want is sex. My heart has been broken one too many times, and at this point, I've given up on true love. My friends have all found it, but not me. I'm calling my move to New York a new start. I'm living for me this time, and no one else.

Ugh. I'm such a hypocrite. I was eyeballing Julius the other night like he was a piece of meat. I listened to everything he said to people, but the whole time, I was undressing him with my eyes. Isn't that acting just like the guys I hate? But he's absolutely gorgeous, and I like this flame he's lit inside me.

It's been a long time since I've felt any excitement on a sexual level. When I handed him that glass of water and our fingers touched, the most amazing heat shot through every cell of my body. Of course, it was quickly extinguished by the water. It was hard to sleep that night because I couldn't stop fantasizing about what it'd feel like if more than our fingers touched.

It's Sunday, and I haven't seen or heard from him. Why would I anyway? Daisy's my contact. I spoke to her yesterday, but it was purely business. Maybe because Monica was still there when Daisy called. She left late last night, and I'm glad. I'm exhausted from this weekend.

Lacey pokes me. "Hey—where'd you go? I'm talking and it's like you aren't even here."

"Shit. I'm sorry. I guess I'm more tired than I realized. Here, let me show you my office. I still need to decorate or get a plant to add some color." I'm babbling and I know it.

Lacey shakes her head. "Where is the Skylar I know? This office is neat and organized. My apartment—I mean *your* apartment—looked like something exploded and you left everything where it landed the last time I was there."

"I know! Aren't you proud of me? I'm trying. I need to keep my ducks in a row here. Maybe it will spread to the apartment."

We sit in the office for a while, drinking coffee, chatting about the opening, and how Julius showed up unexpectedly. I give them a rundown on the type of person he is.

"Oh, let me show you the first article and review that was published yesterday. I was so nervous about what they'd say." I pull up the website, then turn my laptop to face them.

Lacey points to Julius in the picture. "So that's the photographer? *Jeez*. He needs to learn how to smile or to relax. His face is so rigid, he looks like he's got a stick up his ass."

"Hey, be nice. He's not used to having his picture taken. You should see him in person." *Why am I defending him?* "I think he underestimated what he'd be dealing with. Anyway, it doesn't matter because the article and review are glowing. Monica's on cloud nine. His agent, Daisy, was thrilled and relieved. She would've had to deal with his wrath if something had gone wrong."

"And you're on cloud nine too. For more reasons than one," Lacey points out. She has a glint in her eye like she knows something I don't.

A big smile grows on my face. "I really am. I worked my ass off for this opening, and it was more successful than I could've imagined. Monica praised me the entire time, and that pushed my confidence to a whole new level."

I change the subject so they don't get bored of me babbling about this anymore. Lacey tells me that Sophia's sister and parents are coming from Germany in August. It's the first time the families will meet. Jocelyn and Christian have offered to have a big barbecue when they arrive.

"I'd better be invited. I need some family time. They didn't mention it on Friday night."

"Of course you are. Jocelyn just told me this morning. And why would they have mentioned it on Friday? That was your night."

I shrug. "So how is Josh doing? I hope he's treating the ladies well. If he's not, I'm going to have to make a special trip to the marina to kick his ass." I miss him. He's such a goof, but a major player.

Will looks at his vibrating phone and huffs. "Speaking of Josh, I need to call him."

I stand up. "You can have my office. Lacey and I can chat in the front. Take your time and don't forget to finish your cappuccino. Tell him I said hi."

Lacey and I wander through the showroom while she looks at the photographs again, pointing out the ones she likes.

"I hate it that we don't have a lot of time to talk anymore. Jocelyn mentioned some heated tension between you and this angry but gorgeous photographer." She waggles her eyebrows. "How do you plead?"

I roll my neck and growl. "Guilty. He has me in knots, and I don't even know him. Well, I know the photographer side of him, but that isn't much. He's very cryptic. Just looking at him gets me on edge. Or maybe I'm desperate. I can't tell you how damn hard it was for me to remain professional the entire time he was here!"

"Ooh la la. So what are you going to do about it?"

I rub my hands together. "I don't know. I promised myself I wouldn't get involved with anyone for at least six months when I moved here. My heart can't take another letdown. But who knows—I'm probably talking about something that isn't even there. Not to mention, there's business between us. And I don't know what his relationship is with his agent."

Lacey's phone rings. She pulls it out of her back pocket. "Sorry. Let me get this. It's someone from the marina. Don't they know Will is on the phone with Josh?" I nod and she walks to a quiet corner. "What? I can't hear you?" She heads back to me. "The reception's bad. I'll take it outside."

I check the messages on my phone while I wait for them. Nothing. Who am I expecting a message from on a Sunday?

Will's voice sounds from my office. "Shit!" Now what? I find him frantically wiping coffee off my desk with tissues.

"What happened?"

"Somehow the cup slipped from my fingers. I caught it, but I've got coffee all over my shirt and on your desk." I walk around him to see.

"That's not just a little bit." I laugh. "You're going to stink in this hot weather. Do you have another shirt in your backpack?"

"Funny enough, I do. Let's clean this up, then I'll change quickly." We wipe up the rest of the coffee, then walk out to the front where his bag is.

"Where's Lacey?"

"Someone called from the marina. Reception is bad in here, so she went outside."

"The one day we take off, and all hell breaks loose."

He pulls his shirt off and rummages through his backpack.

"Do you always have a spare shirt with you?"

"No. But I have to go straight to work, and I wanted to wear one of the marina shirts. Good thing."

Frantic barking grabs Will's and my attention. I jump and glance out the window. Julius is standing in front of the entrance with Chance. He's wearing a light blue button-down and khaki shorts. Nice change from black and white. My skin tingles, and my face suddenly flushes. He doesn't look happy when he glances at Will and then back at me. Julius, not Chance. Chance's tail is whipping fast enough that it'd leave a mark on someone's skin. I look back at Will, and he swiftly puts his shirt on.

"I'm sorry, Sky. I forgot where I was. I should've changed in the bathroom."

"It's fine. The gallery's closed."

"Who's that guy? I don't like the way he's looking at us."

"Well, I kinda don't blame him. You're standing there half-naked. People might get the wrong idea. But I can take care of myself. You don't recognize him from the picture I just showed you? He has sunglasses on now so maybe you wouldn't. That's the photographer, Julius. I wonder why he's here."

The real question should be, how did he know I was here?

Julius's jaw ticks as usual. Lacey returns and stands behind him at an angle where I can see her. She says something to him. He looks at me once more, then backs up from the door. His body is tight, like every muscle is cramped. Lacey bends over to pet Chance, but he snaps at her. She jerks her hand away and swings the door open. Julius tugs on Chance's leash and mumbles something.

"That dog's crazy," she exclaims. "He almost bit me. Is that Julius? He's way too intense."

"Yes. Give me a second."

Julius moves away from the door as I walk toward it. Why does he look so pissed off? Is it because of Will? Wait a second… is he jealous?

Chance's tail is wagging so hard that he can't control his backside. I open the door, and he bolts toward me. I pet his head and stoop to his level. He licks me more than he did the other day, and props his front paws on my shoulders. I lose my balance but catch myself with my hand on the sidewalk. "Hi, sweet thing. At least you look happy to see me. Can I get up now before I fall on my butt again?" Julius pulls lightly on his leash, but Chance doesn't budge.

"Down, buddy," that sexy voice says. "Come here."

I stand up and wipe down my white capris that now have paw prints on them. "Chance seems happy to see me, but you don't. Why is that?"

His jaw ticks again. Don't hate me, but he's so hot when he does that.

"Did I interrupt you? It looked like you were busy," he responds dryly.

My head jerks back. "And what exactly are you insinuating?"

"Do you always have half-naked guys in the gallery?"

I prop my hands on my hips. "That's none of your business."

"It is when my work is hanging on those walls."

"Seriously?" I snap. "You've got a lot of nerve. You're surrounded by naked women all the time. Have I complained about how you conduct your business? If anything, I'm promoting it."

A group of people come up behind me. We step to the side so they can move around us. I should lower my voice anyway.

"Look, we're getting nowhere with this conversation, and I don't need this right now. If you aren't going to tell me why you're here, then I'm going back inside." Seconds pass in silence. Only the noise of cars zipping by and the conversation of random pedestrians fills the air. I've had enough of this. "You're a man of few words, Julius. It's always a pleasure. Bye, Chance." I turn to leave.

"Wait— Please." I freeze just before I open the door. "I wanted to say I'm sorry."

I turn around. "For what?"

"Do we have to do this out here?" Just as he says this, Lacey and Will come outside.

"Sky, is everything okay?" Lacey asks cautiously. Will stands behind her, warning Julian with a mean stare.

"Yes. We're fine. Talking business. Let me introduce you. Julius, this is my sister, Lacey, and her *boyfriend*, Will. Guys, this is Julius, the photographer of this exhibit."

They shake hands. "It's nice to meet you. I love your work," Lacey says.

"Thanks. Nice to meet you too."

"Sky, something's come up. We need to go. I'm sorry it was such a short visit. At least we'll see you at the barbecue at Jocelyn and Christian's in August. I can't wait to meet Sophia's sister and parents." She embraces me and whispers, "He's hotter in person. Does Will have to kick his ass, though?" *Will wouldn't stand a chance.*

I shake my head and giggle. "Get out of here. Talk to you soon." Will shakes Julius's hand again, and we say goodbye. Julius's body relaxes a bit. Is it because they're gone or because now he knows Will isn't my boyfriend? Why would he care either way? It kills me to admit it, but I know I'll be disappointed if he has a girlfriend.

"So are you coming in?" I open the door. "If you are, leave the attitude at the curb. I've had my limit for the day."

A little smirk grows on his face. "What about Chance? Can I bring him inside?"

"Dogs aren't allowed." I tilt my head and look down at the little charmer. "Will he sit still if I let him in? I'd hate to see the new floors scratched. Monica would have my head."

"He'll behave. I have some treats in my pocket."

I glance at his pockets, then quickly at what's in between. "I'm sure you do." He cocks his head. "Come on in, tough guy. I want to hear this apology. It'd better be good."

10

JULIUS

I saw where her eyes hovered, and it's good that it was a quick glance. No need to embarrass myself by showing her what she does to me. She holds the door open for us to go through.

"Let's go back to my office," she says. "I'd rather Chance hang out back there." Once we're inside, she locks the door.

Chance roams around, sniffing the floor and benches spread throughout the showroom. *Please don't pee on anything, dog!* I remove my sunglasses and hang them on my shirt collar.

"It's amazing how big this place is without people in it," I say to fill the silence. Skylar stands next to one of the leather benches with one knee propped on it.

"I'm surprised you're here—the gallery is closed on Sundays. I was only here because Lacey and Will were stopping by. You're lucky you came when you did. A few minutes later and I would've been gone."

"I just took a chance that you'd be here. It was a long shot, but I lucked out."

"Hopefully, that's a good thing. Stepping out of your comfort zone is never easy or a bad thing. You never know where it can lead you."

"I did that on Friday and survived. And somehow, it led me here today."

A tiny smile lifts her lips. "Would you like a cappuccino, an espresso? Maybe a glass of water?" She leads us to her office. "How about Chance? I can put some water in a mug. I don't have any bowls handy."

"Um, yeah. Sure." She's too nice to me.

"For you or Chance or both?" She looks over her shoulder and I have to blink. Her smile is breathtaking. My heart pounds in my chest, and my throat goes dry. "Water for both of us. Thanks."

"Sure. Sparkling or still?" She looks down at Chance, who's following her around the office. "I don't think you drink seltzer. Regular tap water, right?" *Woof.* "That's what I thought." Now I can't help but smile.

From the doorway, I inspect her office. I didn't really notice much about it on Friday. There was too much going on in here then to look around. To the left is a neat, L-shaped white desk. It's clean of business clutter and personal stuff. Two guest chairs stand in front of it. To the right is a large countertop with water bottles, glasses, cups, and a coffee maker. The walls are bare and aren't the stark white that's in the showroom. They might be a shade of gray.

I try to keep my eyes off her perfect ass in the white pants she's wearing. I like that she's not too skinny. So many of the models who audition for my photo shoots look nearly anorexic. There's nothing wrong with some meat on a woman's bones. That's what gives them the sensual curves I need for my photos.

"Sit down and relax. Here's your water." She motions me to a seat and places a full glass on a coaster nearby. Then she hands me a full mug for Chance. I place it on the floor next to the chair, but wait for her to sit down. As soon as we're seated, Chance trots over and starts lapping up the water. I take a couple of small dog biscuits from my pocket.

"It's amazing how Chance reacts to you. He doesn't warm up to strangers. To anyone, really. Other than me and Daisy and one of my assistants, he snaps and growls. But you—he went straight to you."

"He sounds like someone else in this room," she mutters.

I avoid looking at her because she's right. I can hear the smile in her voice, though. She clears her throat. "How did he lose his leg?"

"I don't know. Somebody found him injured, bleeding, and on the brink of death. Took him to the vet. They don't know what happened but once he healed, the vet sent him to the pound. About six months ago, I decided to get a dog, so I went looking at the pound. I asked them which dog had been there the longest. They introduced me to Chance. He was still in the kennel, but we clicked. He was so excited, jumping around and barking. I couldn't not take him home with me. So we left together. He's been stuck to my hip ever since."

Like he knows we're talking about him, Chance

chooses that moment to jump into my lap. The chair isn't really big enough for the two of us, but we manage. I feed him the treats.

I look back and am surprised to see Skylar gazing at me. She has the cutest expression on her face, and her light-colored eyes glisten. "That was the sweetest story I've ever heard. Julius, I just might start to like you. Why the name Chance?"

"Because everybody deserves a chance, no matter how broken they are."

Silence follows as we observe each other. That sentence was not only about Chance. It was also about me.

I break eye contact and notice the container full of rubber bands on the corner of her desk. "I think you owe me a better apology too."

She perks up. "Excuse me? I haven't even heard one from you yet." Does she have a Boston accent? Something to ask. "What did I do to you?"

I take a rubber band out and stretch it in her direction. I let it go—accidentally, really!—and it bounces off her boob. She releases a soft gasp, then starts laughing. She shoots it back with horrible aim, and it flies over my shoulder. I lift my hands and try not to laugh. Chance jumps off my lap.

"I'm sorry. That wasn't on purpose. Well, okay, maybe it was, but I didn't mean to hit you there." My cheeks feel warm. Am I blushing?

"Huh. So you can be playful. You even laugh and smile. Who'd have known it?" She squints, then props her chin on her clasped hands. "What else are you hiding behind that wall of yours?"

Time to change the subject.

"The reason I came today was to apologize for the way I treated you at the park. I was an asshole. Then I showed up at the opening without announcing it. That was very unprofessional. I shouldn't have played with you like that." I toss my hands up. "And then the way I acted when I arrived today. I'm sorry."

"So why did you?"

I'm suddenly nervous. I jump to my feet. Startled, she leans back in her chair, eyes wide.

"Are you all right?"

"Yeah. Sorry." I wipe my hands on my shorts. "Do you feel like taking a walk? There's a dog park not too far from here. Or we could go back to Central Park. It shouldn't be too crowded today. Chance needs to run around a bit. Do you like ice cream? We can get some before we go to the park." *Stop babbling!*

She smiles. "Did you say ice cream? My stomach growls as I speak. Let's go."

Relief spreads through me. "Good. Come on, Chance." I'm not ready to answer her questions, but I also don't want to walk away from her yet.

11

SKYLAR

I have to be patient and remember that privacy is important to him. If I want to get to know him, I have to let him take the lead. It sounds like a tiny part of his wall has been chipped off since we met on Wednesday. I'm starting to think I'm becoming more interested in the man than the photographer.

"Mint chocolate chip and mango. That is disg—"

"Delicious," I cut him off. "Dark chocolate and vanilla is so boooring." Him and his black and white things. He needs to expand his horizons a bit.

His phone rings. "Can you hold the leash, please?" I take it from his hand so he can take his phone out of his pocket. Chance is busy sniffing and peeing on plants.

"Hey. What's up?" he says to whoever is on the other end. My ear grows several sizes so I can hear what he's saying. Is he talking to a woman?

"I'm in Central Park." He glances at me. "Yes, I'll be back soon. I will when I get the chance. Okay, I'm going.

I thought you had something important to say." He laughs. "See you later." He cuts the call. *Was it Daisy?*

"Want to sit on the grass in the shade over there?" I point to a cute section where there aren't a lot of people but a lot of flowers. It's early evening but it's still warm in the sun.

"Sure." He tries to take the leash back. I pull my arm out of reach and shake my head.

"I've got him. He seems to trust me." And at that precise moment of balancing my ice cream cup and changing the leash from one hand to the other, Chance moves away, jerking my hand and knocking the cup out of it. We both stand there in shock, staring at the upside-down cup on the ground. Then at the same time, we burst out laughing. "What the hell was that? Why are we always dropping stuff when we're together? My poor ice cream. It was so delicious." Chance licks it like he's never eaten before, and Julius takes the leash from me. And I wonder aloud, "Is this what it's like to have children?"

"I'm so sorry, Skylar." He passes his cup to me, then scoops the remaining ice cream back into my cup. Chance looks up at him, licking his chops full of mango ice cream. Julius isn't amused.

"That was the second time you knocked something over that was Skylar's, Chance. You'd better behave, or she won't want to hang out with us again. Do you want that? I sure as hell don't."

Okay, I just melted like my ice cream in the sun. He's so unexpected. Nothing like he was last Wednesday. What else will I learn about him? He walks over to a trash can and throws the ice cream away. Then he comes back and reclaims his cup.

"Julius," I say. He looks my way. "You can call me Sky. That's what my family and friends call me. Skylar's too formal… too businesslike."

He rubs the back of his neck. *What did I say?*

"I thought this was a business meeting?"

My stomach drops and my cheeks start to burn. And then he says, "Sky… I'm just kidding."

I exhale deeply. "That was mean. You had me there for a second."

I almost smacked his arm playfully, but thought better of it. I'm hesitant to touch him. For one, I don't think he's the type, and two, I'm nervous about what'll happen if we do touch. Will it be like the other night when his fingers slid against mine and he dropped the glass?

"Come on. Let's sit down," I suggest. Once my butt hits the ground, I pat the grass next to me. He follows, always careful not to let go of Chance's leash or his ice cream. We stretch our legs out in front of us and enjoy the sunshine. "I am a little confused about why you came to the opening."

"I knew you were the one working with Daisy."

"You mean you knew when we met the first time? How's that possible?"

I glance at his profile as he looks straight ahead. I can almost hear his brain working. He proceeds to tell me how he overheard the conversation I had with Daisy on the phone. Then explains how he observed Daisy and me in the gallery. Why am I not bothered by this? He sounds like a stalker.

I turn my body so I'm facing his side and cross my legs. "Wait, you mean the dog barking outside the gallery was Chance? Daisy was acting really weird at that moment. Did she know you were there?" He shakes his head and focuses on me.

"Not at the time. I had to know if it was you. The curiosity would've eaten me alive."

I need something to do, so I rip some grass out of the ground and play with it in my hands. I'm amazed at how honest he's being, but I want to hear more.

"That still doesn't answer why you came."

"You know the Mossi Krelo Gallery?"

Okay. Random. I toss the grass to the side. "I'd hope so—they're one of the best in the city."

"They contacted Daisy and want to show one of my collections."

"Holy shit! Congratulations. That's awesome! You must be thrilled."

"Yeah… But I have to agree to attend the opening to clinch the deal."

"Oh. But what does that have to do with my gallery?"

"I needed to see what an opening of my work would be like." He shrugs, then his voice becomes serious. "At least that's what I told myself. And what I told Daisy that night. It was a good excuse."

"Excuse? I don't get it." I lean in closer. "Please tell me."

"I wanted to see you."

Suddenly, a butterfly flutters around us and lands on my arm. "Oh my gosh! This is amazing. It's a Buckeye Butterfly. Isn't it beautiful?" It stays there for a few seconds to let us observe it.

He has a pensive smile on his face. "My mom loved butterflies. She was obsessed with a butterfly bush we had in our small backyard. She'd get so excited when she'd see one. Unfortunately, there wasn't much else that made her happy." He talks about her in the past tense. Maybe she died?

"They're beautiful. Especially the ones with blue on their wings." And just like that, it flies away.

"It's not as pretty as your name. It's unique. Sky fits you, because you light up the sky with your presence." He's being goofy but I like it. He tries so hard to act like a tough guy, then he says these things. He's a big pussycat.

"Yeah, well I can darken it too, if someone pisses me off." I narrow my eyes at him. "Beware."

"Good to know."

"Who you see right now is me—Sky. A new friend or acquaintance, whatever you want to call me, but not a business associate. But I need to know who I'm sitting with right now. Julius the photographer or just Julius?"

"It's just me. Even though I'd love to get you in front of my camera one day." He chuckles, and I see red.

"*Excuse me?* Is that why you're being nice all of a sudden? So I'll agree to be one of your models or objects?" I stand up and pat down the back of my pants vigorously.

He jumps up. "Wait a second. What did I say? That was a compliment."

"Maybe to you. Is that all you see? My body?"

"Sky, I didn't mean anything disrespectful by it. Look at you." He motions to my entire body. "You're a beautiful woman. I told you that before, and you didn't get pissed off then."

"Well, I don't want to be a part of your black and white world. When guys look at me, most of them just see my body. Yes, I have curves and boobs, but that's not all I am. I want you to see the real me and not look at me as one of your many models."

He rakes his hand through his hair, then walks over to the nearest tree. After he wraps Chance's long leash around it, he stomps back over to me, his hands balled into fists. I don't know what to expect at this point. He blurts out, "The problem is, I can't see the real you, and you have no fucking clue how frustrating that is."

12

JULIUS

Her forehead crinkles. "What? I don't understand. What do you mean?"

"I'm color-blind, damn it."

"A lot of people are color-blind," she counters. "So you don't see all the colors. You can still see some. What does that have to do with me?"

"You don't get it. I have the rarest form of color blindness you can have. It's called achromatopsia. I can only see black, gray, white, and slight shades in between. Every time I see you, I practically get a headache from willing my eyes to see your true colors. To see you the way everyone else sees you. I'm fucking jealous of those people. I came to terms a long time ago with my inability to see properly. It was my norm. But when you walked into my life, you changed everything." I move a step closer to her, my eyes never leaving hers. My chest heaves.

"You want to know why I acted the way I did the first day I saw you? It's because you're the most beautiful woman I've ever seen, and my wall shot up even higher. That wall is thick and it's up for a reason. But you give off this energy that's making it crumble. And then when you opened your damn gorgeous mouth and let me have it the other day, I was a goner. I'm drawn to you like… like an insect to a flame. I know that's not the best way to say it. I'm not a man of many words and I'm not used to talking to women… Or wanting one so much."

She inches toward me, her light-colored eyes glistening with tears, until we're centimeters apart. Her heavy breathing matches my own.

"I dropped that glass of water on Friday night because of this." I wrap my hand around the back of her neck and capture her mouth with mine. She gasps, then melts into me as I tickle her soft lips with mine. "You feel it, don't you? The way our bodies react to each other." I tease her lower lip with my tongue, and she eagerly responds, entwining hers with mine. She wraps her arms around my neck, and I stroke her back with my free hand.

The hectic world around us disappears.

A delicious hint of mint dances in my mouth and the warm vanilla scent of her hair heightens my senses. She pulls away with hooded eyes and grins. "Wow."

"Hmm mmm. That wasn't enough." I cup her face and kiss her deeper until she consumes my every breath. Electric heat thrums through my body, making me wish we were somewhere else. I'll enjoy this moment of euphoria as long as it lasts, because I don't know if I'll ever get the chance again.

Woof! Woof! Chance nips on my shorts.

Our lips separate slowly. She rests her head in the crook of my neck as she catches her breath. Her left hand rests on my chest.

"I've done so many things out of character since Wednesday, but I'll keep doing them if it means I'll get to see you again." I squeeze her to my side.

She lifts her head, then presses her fingers lightly against my lips where I can still taste her. "Shhh. Let me enjoy this moment because it was absolutely breathtaking. And now, I'm going to leave on this high note and hope you'll watch me walk away."

With my thumb, I caress her cheek, then kiss her nose. "Do you live far from here?"

Her hand embraces mine and squeezes. "I told you not to talk." We laugh. "I'll be fine. Take Chance home." She lets go and pats him on the head. "Bye, Chance. See ya around, Julius. Thanks for the ice cream. You know where to find me."

She grabs her handbag off the ground and walks away. I watch her until she's almost out of sight. She turns and waves, then disappears. I kneel down next to Chance, who has to be exhausted and starving by now. "You like her don't you?"

Woof!

"Yeah, me too. It scares the shit out of me."

"Good. I'll see you tomorrow." I cut the call and put my phone on the table.

"Knock, knock," Daisy says, standing in the doorway to my office.

"Come in." I don't look up as she approaches me.

"Are you going to hide in here with your cameras for the rest of the night? The studio is set up for tomorrow's shoot if you want to check it out."

"Thanks. Look at the camera I'm going to buy." I turn my laptop so she can see the image.

"Like you need another one." She leans forward. "Eight thousand dollars! Are you crazy? Wait a second. I know what's going on here. When you're stressed or have something on your mind, you buy new cameras or equipment. What's up? I should've known—you've been so quiet since you got back after seeing Skylar."

"Cameron's going to stick around for a while after the shoot tomorrow. I want to teach him a few things."

"Okay. Stop avoiding whatever this is."

I close my laptop and spin in my chair toward my sister. "I told her I'm color-blind."

She sits down on the stool next to my desk. "Wow. You hardly know her! You've never told anyone this before. Other than our dead family members, your teachers, and your doctor, I'm the only one who knows. Can you trust her not to tell anyone?"

"To her, it's not a big deal. She doesn't understand why I don't tell anyone. And yeah, I'm sure she'll ask questions that'll dig up the past. I'm not sure I'll ever be ready to answer them, but maybe it's time. I've avoided it up until now."

"But why did you tell her? Why her? What makes her so special?"

"I made a comment about wanting to take pictures of her, and she got so pissed. She wants me to see her, not her beauty, she says. I'm probably not saying it right. I admit it—I can't take my eyes off her, but that's not the only thing. She's the first woman I've actually *seen* in such a long time. Women come and go during my shoots, and I don't miss them when they're gone. I pay attention to them through my lens as objects, not people. She's the first woman I want to take pictures of *and* get to know as a person. I want to take shots of her throughout the day; I want to catch every emotion. I want to show her exactly how I see her. I don't want to tie her up in a knot so she looks like a mountain peak."

"How did you end it today?"

I take a deep breath, wondering if I should tell her. She's the only one I can talk to and is basically my best friend. But I never discuss the women I date with her.

I'm quiet long enough that she takes a guess. Her eyes are wide. "You kissed her. Or she kissed you." I lift my head, and I guess my expression gives it away. A big smile grows on her face. "Tell me. Who kissed who?"

"I kissed her, and damn if it wasn't the best thing I've ever experienced. I don't know what the hell got into me. My control snapped, and I had to know what she tastes like or feels like under my embrace. Chance interrupted us… which was probably for the better since we were in the middle of the park. She walked off with a smile on her face, and that was it."

"You didn't talk about meeting again? Nothing?"

I shake my head. "She said I know where to find her."

"Holy shit! She's giving you the opening. Wait. Did you at least tell her I'm your sister? Or what your real name is?"

"No. I never had the time."

She lets out a long sigh. "Why not?"

"We were distracted by something around us or Chance. Or each other." I can't help the silly grin on my face.

She pats my knee. "We always knew, one day, one of us would meet someone special, someone who'll love us despite our baggage. If you think Skylar could be that person, then you need to tell her everything so she can understand why you are the way you are. And even if it ends up not being her, we're going to have to talk about our past someday. We can't pretend and hide behind the cameras and tattoos our whole lives. We've done it for so long… but we've wasted a lot of precious time. Life is really good right now, and we've worked hard for it, so we shouldn't let those horrific memories of our father have control over us anymore."

"Your therapist is doing a good job. I've never seen you so free before. I'm proud of you. Maybe I should be going with you."

She crosses her arms. "Right. I tell you all the time to come, but no. You're a tough guy, and tough guys don't need therapy."

"I have Chance. He's my therapy dog."

"Whatever." She stands up. "Want Skylar's number?"

"No. I'm going to handle this my own way."

13

SKYLAR

I've called an emergency meeting with Sophia and Jocelyn. With their crazy work schedules, we've agreed to meet early for breakfast this morning. I would've loved to sleep in, but I can't stop thinking about that kiss yesterday. I can't keep it to myself.

There they are. I wave to them as they walk through the door of the café. They each flash me a smile and approach the table. I stand up and give them hugs.

Once we sit down and get comfortable, I say, "I'm so glad you both could come. I really need some girl time. I just wish Lacey could be here too."

"I don't have class until eleven on Mondays," Sophia says. "I can't wait to hear what's going on. How could you call us and not tell us what this is about?"

"It better be about that grouchy hot photographer," Jocelyn teases. "If not, I'm grabbing a bagel to go, and I'm out of here."

"Nah, you want to stay," I tell her. "But let's order

first. I need a caffeine injection—I only had a couple hours of sleep."

"Holy shit! Did you sleep with him?" Jocelyn's excited voice travels through the small café. A woman at the table next to us chokes on her orange juice. Jocelyn claps a hand over her mouth. "I'm so sorry."

"Well, that was embarrassing." Sophia hides behind her menu and sinks in her chair.

"The quicker we order, the faster I'll tell you." They both slap their menus closed. Boy, are they eager. Jocelyn waves a waitress over and we place our orders.

Then they lean in over the table with anticipation in their eyes.

"You guys!" I protest. "Now you're making me feel bad. Maybe it isn't as exciting as you think. And no, I didn't sleep with him."

"So it is about him! Julius Ariti. The Greek god himself." Jocelyn cheers.

"Yes. Now be quiet so I can tell you the story." The waitress approaches with our drinks. I make space for my coffee. We take our first sips, then I wrap my hands around the hot cup. "So this is what happened yesterday." I spend the next several minutes telling them the long version of the story this time, about Chance banging into me. After a lot of questions, I move on to yesterday.

"So you're saying he was angry about Will being shirtless?" Jocelyn laughs. "He's jealous. He might've thought you were going at it in the back. I'd probably come to the same conclusion if a topless woman showed up next to Christian."

"A topless woman is totally different than a topless man. But whatever. It's not the point. Once I introduced them, he relaxed and was in a better mood."

The waitress brings our food. I look at my cheese and tomato egg white omelet and suddenly lose my appetite. Talking about Julius gives me butterflies and makes me nervous... in a good way.

"Move on with the story," Jocelyn orders. "I don't care if you have a mouthful of food."

"Jeez, girl! You're so aggressive this morning." Sophia laughs. "What's up with you?"

"Ugh! There's just so much love in the air this year. First you and Drew, then Lacey and Will, now Sky. I guess I am a bit overexcited. Sorry. Move on." Love's in the air? She's nuts.

I tell them how Julius rescued Chance and what he said—*Everybody deserves a chance, no matter how broken they are.*

"Aww." Jocelyn crosses her arms on the table and leans forward. "That's almost poetic. He's such a private person... maybe he isn't only talking about Chance. Maybe he's broken too, and that's why he's such an introvert."

I rest my chin on my hand thoughtfully. "That's possible. I wanted to know what's behind his wall and why he showed up at the gallery again, and as soon as I asked, he hopped up and suggested we go for a walk."

"Did you go? Or did he leave?"

Sophia squeezes Jocelyn's hand. "I'm going to tape your mouth shut if you don't let Sky finish her story."

"Ha! Look who's aggressive now. But fine. I'll keep

my questions until the end, but it won't be easy." She shoves part of her bagel into her mouth.

Finally I tell them about his unexpected kiss that almost dropped me to my knees, and how it shattered my vow to avoid men. Both of them sit there staring at me, to the point I'm uncomfortable.

"Can we talk now?" Jocelyn asks, putting her glass down.

"Yes." I cut into my now cold omelet and eat a tiny bite, then wash it down with coffee.

They start babbling like chickens. They repeat what I just told them like I'm not even here. I did leave out that he's color-blind. My gut says not to tell them. It's not something he talks about. Otherwise, I'm sure I would've read about it when I researched him. I know I can trust them, but it doesn't feel right.

"Ladies! I'm still at the table. Talk to *me*." They both jump and start laughing. They're in good moods for a Monday morning.

"You know, even though he has that abrasive side, he's really into you. You shouldn't be mad that he'd like to take pictures of you. He just wants you to know how beautiful you are. Nothing you've said makes me think he only wants to get you into bed," Jocelyn explains. "Also, he's doing business with you. He doesn't want to screw up his or your image. Imagine—he's always so private, but then he shows up at an opening and some big scandal breaks out. You know what I mean?"

Sophia shakes her head. "That's not going to happen. If he didn't have strong feelings for you, he would've stayed away and never revealed himself."

Jocelyn raises her finger. "Side question. What is the relationship between Daisy and Julius? Anything romantic there?"

"I have no idea. I only saw them together at the opening. She gave me no reason to think they were ever involved. She did say she's known him forever. Maybe they went to school together. I asked her questions about him before I knew who he was, but her mouth was always sealed. She didn't reveal anything."

"Does she know that you were with him yesterday?"

I shrug my shoulders. "I have no idea. I don't want to get her involved, in case this goes down the drain. Things would get really uncomfortable then. Of course, now that the opening is over, I won't have as much contact with her as I did before. I don't have Julius's phone number. Maybe he'll stop by the gallery this week."

"Can we go back to him taking pictures of you?" Sophia asks between chewing. I nod. "You're not even a little bit curious or interested?"

"Just don't pose nude for him. You never know where those pictures will end up. And don't make a video." Jocelyn leans in and whispers, "Christian and I did it once a long time ago. I was a bit heavier after having Coral. Anyway, I couldn't watch it with all my jiggly bits jiggling. I was horrified. We deleted it immediately. It took me a while to have sex with the lights on again."

Sophia and I look at Jocelyn with our mouths wide open. "Jocelyn!" Sophia exclaims.

"Shush," I say, glancing at the people around us. "We're going to get kicked out of here."

"I just don't see you and Christian as the type to do that. Especially Christian. You kinky girl!" Sophia teases her.

"We might be married for a while now, but the flame is still burning." She clicks her tongue. *Eww!* The only thing I can picture is Christian holding a calculator to add up his investments while they're going at it. Yes, it's bitchy, but sometimes I think he loves his investments more than anything else.

She sees the expression on my face. "What? Anyway, this isn't about my sex life, this is about yours. So is there a tiny bit of interest? Don't you want to see him behind a camera… to see him in action?"

"I love watching Drew make new jewelry pieces," Sophia enthuses. "He's so creative and serious. I wish I could lie in a pool of sapphires…"

"Ouch. That would hurt." Jocelyn elbows Sophia and they chuckle.

I'm distracted by thoughts of a barefoot Julius, shirtless and wearing old, low-hanging jeans that are frayed at the bottom. I wonder if he has tattoos on other parts of his tanned body. I imagine his authoritative voice, telling me how to pose. And then he sets down his camera and comes over to help me get into those positions. *Oh man.* I squeeze my legs together. I have to prevent myself from moaning in the middle of this place.

"So you girls really think I should take things further?"

"Yes," they say in unison.

"If I ever see him again."

"Yes!"

"Oh, I'm sure you'll see him again. Probably sooner than you think," Jocelyn adds, nodding her head emphatically. "And if things progress, invite him to the barbecue in August."

"You're crazy. I think you're getting ahead of yourself. And you never told me about the barbecue. I had to hear about it from Lacey yesterday. I'm offended." I play with her.

"Don't even. Our parents and friends will be there and some of Will's family too, since they're involved in the wedding. I can't wait."

And finally, the conversation moves on to wedding details, and I don't have to talk about Julius anymore.

That doesn't mean I'm not thinking about him.

14

JULIUS

My palms are sweating, and my heart is pounding. The gallery should be closing soon, and I'm peeking through the windows again, watching Skylar. I'm not stalking her, honestly. Why do I get so nervous when I know I'm going to see her? She's awakened a part of me that wasn't dead yet, but dormant. Foreign emotions flood my body when I'm with her.

Daisy and I both have scars and dark clouds from the past, but we handle our struggles differently. She tried many ways to cope. A lot of them were really bad, but she's found a therapist now that she loves, who has helped immensely. I've seen such a positive change in her these last few years, and she's kicking ass as my agent. I'm proud of her, and I hope her success lasts.

Me, I hide behind my work. For the most part, I've become numb against the pain of my past. I avoid meeting new people so I don't have to talk about myself. When I do venture out, I pretty much just talk about my photography. It's why I use a pseudonym. No one can search me out and learn who I really am.

Skylar has a customer, so I've decided to wait outside. I don't want to interrupt her. When she talks about my photographs, she becomes very animated. Even before I met Skylar, Daisy had told me how much she loves my work. It's a real compliment to see and hear how passionate she is about them.

The woman shakes her hand and walks toward the door. Skylar follows and lets her gaze scan the street outside. Her entire face lights up when she sees me. She opens the door for her customer and says goodbye. I wait a few seconds and then approach her slowly.

She leans against the edge of the door. "Hi," she says, almost melting away. I wish I had my camera—I'd capture the dreamy expression on her face. I have to wonder what's going through her mind. Then she welcomes me with a saucy grin. Warmth spreads through my chest.

"Hi." I find myself smiling back.

"What a nice surprise. I'm just about to close up." She steps to the side to let me in. "How long have you been standing outside in this heat? You should've come in. I could've introduced you to a future fan. She's going to call me tomorrow to let me know whether she wants *The Bow* or not."

A breeze follows me in and circulates her vanilla scent around me. "I still need a break from opening night," I confess.

She closes the door and leans her back against it.

"I'm sure. Where's Chance? He's always glued to your side."

I'm standing in the middle of the gallery, and she chats away like I'm an old friend. I wish it were that easy for me to talk to someone.

"He's at home. I'm sorry to just show up."

"So are you here for personal or business reasons?" She pushes off the door and saunters in my direction.

"Personal."

Her smile grows. "I am admittedly a big fan of your work, but I'd rather talk to *you* than your business side."

"Good. Does that mean you might go to dinner with me, or do you already have plans?"

"I was just going to head to the gym. But I don't need to go."

"You definitely don't." I keep my eyes on her face, but I'm already regretting what I just said. "Sorry. You made it clear you don't like it when someone talks to you like that."

"Julius, relax." She rubs her hands up and down my arms. A warm sensation pumps through my blood, relaxing every muscle except one. Hopefully, she won't notice. "After what you told me the other day, I won't question comments like that. Okay?"

I nod.

"Good. If we go to dinner, can we stop by my apartment first? I'd like to change clothes and shoes and drop off my laptop."

"Sure. Whatever you want. Is it far from here?"

"Only a couple of blocks. I live close enough to the gallery to walk to work. It's a dream, really."

"It's nice to be close to work. My studio is in the same building as my apartment. I've done a few projects at remote locations, but most of my shoots happen in the studio."

"In the same building? I don't know if I'd like *that* or not. I need a little distance and to get some fresh air once in a while, I think." She shrugs. "Can you wait a few minutes while I close things up for the day? Go check out the walls to see which photographs have sold since you were here last. You should be so proud of yourself."

I shove my hands in my pockets. "Take your time. I'm in no rush." And that's true. Chance is with Daisy, so no worries there. I have the whole evening to spend with Skylar. I still need to tell her my real name and that Daisy is my sister. I know I should've told her that already. It's just a name, but I feel bad that I haven't said anything. Like I'm lying. Daisy has purposely put some distance between her and Skylar so I could get to know her.

"Okay. I'm ready. Let's get outta here." There's the accent again.

"Are you from Boston?"

"You heard that? My accent sneaks out here and there."

I follow her out of the gallery and wait while she locks up.

"Are you embarrassed to have an accent?"

"Not really. Especially here where half the people you meet have accents. But I do notice mine more when

I'm at the gallery. I grew up in Boston—lived there my whole life till a couple of months ago."

"Well, I think it's sexy."

"Sure. Sure. That's what they all say," she jokes, then her handbag falls off her shoulder with a thump, jerking her arm down. Between that and the sweater and the laptop she's juggling, we're about to have another accident.

"Here," I say. "Give me your laptop. I can carry it for you."

"As much as we drop stuff around each other, you think that's safe?" She laughs and hands it over. As she does, someone pushes past us and shoves her into my chest.

I hadn't realized how crowded the sidewalk was or that we were holding up traffic. I've got my free arm around her now, though, so I'm not going to complain. In fact, I might take advantage of it.

Her lips are inches away. I reach up and caress her cheek with my thumb. Seconds tick by like nothing around us exists.

Another jostle from the crowd and she pulls away. "I like how you feel against me, but we're in the way. Come on, Mr. Camera Man."

We walk the few blocks to her apartment with her chatting about her day and how many customers came to the gallery. It's been busier than they expected, apparently.

"Monica and I were thinking it'd be best to wait awhile to hire someone, at least until we see if the gallery's a success. Now, I don't want to wait because then I'm working all the time. What if I get sick or need a day off? There's no one to back me up."

She stops and pulls some keys out of her bag. "This is my building. Wanna come up? I have to warn you, my place is a mess. If I knew I'd have company, I would've straightened up a bit."

"I'm sure it's not too bad, but you *are* from Boston. You never know."

She slaps my arm. "Real nice. Something tells me that you're Mr. Orderly and everything is sterile in your place. Nothing out of order. I can't even imagine what your equipment or storage room looks like. You seem to need to be in control, to have everything your way. No surprises. Like with your photo displays. It's your defense. I bet the only thing that gets away with being messy is Chance."

I'm speechless because she's right. She turns to look at me.

"So? How did I do? Am I right? Especially for someone who doesn't know you very well? I'm good at reading people, so beware."

She steps backward to the door behind her. I follow until she's pressed up against it. I plant my hands on the sides of her head and lean in.

"I'll confess that you're one hell of a surprise. And I've survived so far." I lean in closer as my eyes memorize the curve of her face. "There's no controlling you, but I don't want to. And I still keep coming back." Our lips are dangerously close. Her breathing increases. "I want to kiss you," I say softly. She lifts her chin in encouragement. "But not against this dirty door."

She huffs and presses her hand on my chest. "You're such a tease. Who would've thought you'd be so playful."

"I'm usually not. That's until you came along. Let's get back to messy. You've looked beautiful every time I've seen you… but maybe I need to see your apartment first. I might have to skip dinner." A contagious laugh bursts out from within her, and I find myself doing the same.

Once we get to her apartment, she unlocks the door and we step in. I remove my sunglasses. This might be the only time I've ever been glad to be color-blind. With the number of different shades of gray, I have a feeling this room is an explosion of color. Straight ahead is the living room. On the coffee table is a laundry basket, overflowing with clothes. Clean or not? Don't know. Pillows from the couch are on the floor next to a couple of magazines and sneakers. A blanket sits in a ball on the couch along with a pair of jeans. A towel hangs over the armrest.

She places the laptop on the kitchen table to the right of the living room. A couple of black bras hang off one of the chairs. She snatches them up and tosses them in the laundry basket. Maybe they aren't black. I wish I could see their color. But then again, black is always sexy.

"Sorry." She shrugs and grins confidently at me. I love it that she doesn't give a shit. "I warned you. It's a big difference from the gallery office." She grabs the basket and walks toward a hallway. "I'm going to get changed. Give me a few minutes. Make yourself at home."

"I'll be here."

"There are some art magazines on the floor by the couch. Oh, and there's an awesome review about the opening if you haven't seen it yet. It's on the kitchen table." I hear a door close.

"Get dressed," I shout. "I'm hungry. Think about what you want to eat."

I could swear she just said *you*. But maybe that was just me.

"Sushi?" she calls out.

There was a time I thought I'd never let sushi pass my lips, but then I lost a bet to Daisy. I had to eat it. It's been an addiction ever since.

"Sounds good." I walk through the living room and snoop around. There's a container full of rubber bands on the coffee table. What kind of fetish is this? I chuckle to myself.

I scan the pictures on her shelves. There's one of Skylar with an older woman in a simple wedding dress. It could be her mom. Skylar looks gorgeous. In another picture, I recognize her sister, Lacey, the one I met at the gallery the other day. And Sky is in a string bikini that does very little to cover up her perfect breasts. My mouth goes dry. She is by far the sexiest woman I've ever met. Why do I have to be color-blind? I'd do anything to see the colors of her bikini, her flawless skin, her hair, and the color of her gorgeous eyes, reflecting off the ocean.

I look a little closer. The two guys in the picture look

like twins. One is next to Skylar and the other is next to her sister. They look like the shirtless guy at the gallery. Lacey's boyfriend. I cringe, thinking about how jealous I was when I saw him through the window.

A cloud of Skylar's fresh vanilla scent fills the air around me. "That's Lacey," she says. "You met her on Sunday. And Will and Josh. They're twins. Ready to go?"

I turn around and take a step back. *Blink, blink.* "Wow… You're stunning." Her hair is pulled up with tendrils falling around her face. My lips ache to kiss her bare neck. She's wearing a light-colored, sleeveless long-pants jumpsuit that ties at the ankles. Slits in the fabric expose the skin of her calves. Her strappy shoes show off her toe ring.

She puts her hands on her cheeks. "Stop looking at me like that. You're making me blush." I remove her hands from her face and tug her toward me.

"Why? It's true."

"Show me with a kiss then." *So bossy. I love it.*

Her hypnotizing eyes hold my gaze. I inch closer, then trace her lower lip with my thumb. "What if I can't stop?"

"What if I don't want you to?" One side of her mouth curls up. "If it's anything like the other day…"

This time I'm not going for fast and hard. I want all my heat to transfer to every part of her body. I wrap one arm around her slender waist and gently pull her toward me. I skim my lips over hers, just long enough to tease her. She closes her eyes, and her lips part in anticipation. I'm already hard and I haven't even kissed her yet.

I rest my other hand on her shoulder and rub my thumb below her ear. Her body quivers in response. She licks her lips. "You're killing me."

"That's the purpose."

I kiss the corners of her mouth, then our lips connect. The taste of her is a delicacy. It's a treat every time. Her tongue teases my lips open, searching for mine. And when they connect, taking it slow is history. She wraps her arms around my back, and I let my hands get lost in her hair. I release her wanton mouth and find her soft neck. A gasp escapes from her as I suck, nip and tease from her ear down to her collarbone. Her pulse point races against my needy lips. My desire urges me to move farther down, but I resist.

Grumble. Growl.

I freeze. What the hell?

She giggles, pulls away, and rubs her belly. "Sorry. I'm starving." *So am I.*

Once I can breathe normally, and she fixes her hair, I intertwine my fingers with hers. "Let's get some food in you. I don't want you passing out on me."

"My favorite sushi bar is about a fifteen-minute walk from here. Want to check it out?"

"I'm high on you right now, so I'll do whatever you want."

"Let's see how dinner goes first." She kisses my neck, not knowing that she has me wrapped around her finger already.

An hour later, we're stuffed and sipping on our drinks in a quiet corner, watching sushi dishes pass us on the conveyor belt. We angle our bodies so we can see each other better without cramping our necks. We've been sharing stories.

"So Lacey is actually your stepsister."

"Yes and also one of my best friends. I'm an only child, so when my mom told me she'd met someone and he had a daughter my age, I was really excited. I didn't expect us to become as close as we are, though."

"And her boyfriend… or are they engaged?"

"Boyfriend, but to me they're already married. They're so in love it's sickening. They give me hope, since I've never been lucky in that department. Forever hopeful, but always let down…" She takes a sip of wine. I wonder what that remark was about. Probably the reason she snapped at me the other day. "Guess how long they've been together."

"No clue. You're asking a guy." I rub my chin. "A couple of years?"

She laughs. "Nope. Nearly four months. Love at first sight can do that to you."

Yeah, I know. Wait, no I don't.

"Lacey and I went to St. Thomas in April. Oh, wait!" She grabs my hand, sending tantalizing sparks up my arm that find their way to my pounding heart.

Does she have any clue what she does to me? She's tying me in knots—brain and body. I have to pull myself back to what she was saying. *Love at first sight?* I push it out of my mind.

"Do you remember that snowstorm in April? Apparently it was total chaos here."

"Sure," I say with a scratchy voice. "How could I forget? We were scheduled to shoot *The Wave* and *The*

Bow that week. Several models canceled due to travel issues." I laugh, remembering. "You think I'm a control freak now—you should've seen me that day. But in the end there was nothing I could do. We went ahead with what we had, and the photos came out even better than I expected. It all worked out in the end."

"It sure did, since *The Wave* sold first… just like I said it would." She leans over and kisses my cheek. Her chest rubs against my upper arm. It's good that we're in a public place. I don't know if I could keep my hands off her otherwise, or at least my lips.

"Anyway," she continues, "because of that storm, my flight from Boston to JFK was canceled. Will got my empty seat on the plane from JFK to St. Thomas. I flew down later." She continues to tell me about their trip and how Lacey and Will got together. She's genuinely happy for them. I love listening to her talk when she's passionate about something. I wonder if I talk about my job like that.

"Tell me what colors you are."

"What?" She looks at me quizzically. "What do you mean?"

"Describe what you look like. The color of your hair, your eyes, your skin… I can guess by connecting your colors to other objects, but I want you to tell me. Like my eyes. Everyone says I have brown eyes like chocolate or coffee."

"Hmm. The first time I saw you, I thought dark redwood or a really rich cognac. So beautiful and unique. I've never seen brown eyes with a slightly red tint to them."

Time to open up a bit. I don't want to, but I need to. "The reason they have that tint is because I have to wear special red contacts for my color blindness. My eyes are very sensitive to bright light or sunlight. I wear them during the day and sometimes switch to regular contacts in the evening. When I was much younger and didn't have contacts, I had to wear special sunglasses all the time."

"Even inside?" she asks.

"Yes. Now with these contacts, I'm fine when I'm inside. I only need to wear regular sunglasses in addition to my contacts, outside." She moves closer to me, then searches my eyes.

"Yes, I can see them now. It's so interesting." She leans back. "What about your photo shoots? All those lights…"

"It's not a problem most of the time. If it gets to be too much, then I use my sunglasses. The models look at me funny, but hey. I'm eccentric." I laugh. "I'm actually very lucky because my sensitivity and vision could've been so much worse. These contacts improve my vision drastically, but I'll never have perfect eyesight."

That's enough about me for now. Time to focus on her. I nudge her arm with mine.

"So what color are your eyes? My guess is a light blue or green. But I'm going to go with green."

"Good guess. They're light green… like a four-leaf clover or a lime. Or sometimes like a green apple. The color of my outfit is similar. Lacey always tells me this color looks good with my olive skin."

"Oh, nice. Olive skin?"

"Yes, I have an Italian background. So I have a nice tan all year round." She holds her arm up against mine. Her skin is slightly darker than mine and still sparkles. But it's hard to compare with the hair on my arm. Her skin is flawless. Hardly any freckles or birthmarks.

"When I look at your skin, it sparkles."

"Oh, that's just the body lotion I use." I bite my lip hard to prevent myself from imaging her rubbing the lotion all over her body.

"Good to know. I thought my eyes were playing tricks on me. I never can tell. Anyway, go on."

She glances at her arm. "Right now I have a tan, so I'm a little darker than during the winter months. I wouldn't say my skin is creamy, it's more a bronzed color. Maybe light brown sugar or golden honey." She stops. "This is so difficult. How can you understand me at all if you have never seen colors?"

"I group things together by similar colors. I was born with this, so I have no real clue, but I do see different shades of gray. It's just like a black and white photo. There are different shades and contrasts in the darkness, different depths, and density... For example, I'm told my hair is black. I can see the shade of your hair is lighter, so I know it's not black. I also know it's probably brown, comparing it to someone like Daisy. Her hair looks gray to me, but she calls it silver. When she says silver, I think of silverware or silver jewelry. Your toe ring isn't silver. Most likely, it's gold. Am I right?"

"Yes. I'm surprised you even noticed."

I lean into her. "I notice everything about you,

woman, and it's fucking sexy as hell. And it's only because you're the one wearing it. I've seen other women with them, and I've never really cared. But with you… I can't explain it. It fits your look, and I find it extremely attractive. Just like your tiny nose ring. Or stud? I don't know the lingo when it comes to piercings." I raise an eyebrow. "Do you have any other ones?"

A devilish smirk grows on her face. "Two others."

Damn. I shouldn't have asked that question. My mind spins, imagining all the areas on her body that could be pierced. Which leads to me picturing her stretched out naked on a sheepskin rug in my studio, a simple white sheet covering the most intimate parts of her body. My throat goes desert dry, and my shorts feel snug.

"Want to know where?"

I nod and try to calm my breathing by thinking about nailing a hole in the wall. *Nailing? Hole?* I should just jump into a pool of ice. It's been so long, I can't control myself.

"Here." She points to her earlobes, then bursts out laughing. "You should've seen your face. You have a dirty mind, Mr. Ariti. This could make things very interesting later on."

And just like that, *Ariti* extinguishes any sexual thoughts I have.

I need to tell her the truth about my name and about me and Daisy. I've purposely directed our conversations to be about Skylar so she wouldn't ask me too many questions. The more I'm with her, the more I feel I can trust her, but it's too soon and it's so hard for me to open up.

15

SKYLAR

I f he's good at being in control, I don't know how he does it. My pulse has been racing since he walked through the gallery door tonight. I haven't felt this sensation in so long. And never so intense. Kissing him is like a new art form. His lips are full, soft, and strong, but they're gentle too. His tongue is hot, sweet, and spicy like chocolate and chilis. I can just imagine his tongue on other parts of my body. My belly swirls with excitement.

On our walk back to my apartment, I decide to be brave. Or maybe stupid. "I'm glad you stopped by tonight. I've been thinking about you a lot, and not just because of your photos. It's funny, actually. That's hardly the reason at all." Once the confession is out, I'm suddenly swamped by fear. What if he doesn't feel the same way? I look straight ahead, afraid to see the expression on his face. But really, why should I worry when he's been holding my hand since we left the restaurant? That alone is surprising. I wouldn't have taken him as a hand holder.

In fact, he squeezes my hand now, as he replies. "I know what you mean. You've made it nearly impossible for me to focus on my current project. But you've also helped me come up with a new one."

"I have? Now I'm curious."

"I'm not quite sure how to go about it. It needs work —I've never done anything like it before."

"Do I get a hint, since I inspired you?"

He stops short and brushes his lips across the top of my hand, making me tingle everywhere. "You'll be the first to see it, unless you kick me to the curb by then."

"I can't imagine that. The rumors about you are the opposite of what I see. The last name Ariti means friendly, generous, and approachable. The first time I met you, you were definitely not approachable or friendly, but you proved me and all the rumors wrong. Maybe that's what you want people to see so they'll leave you alone, but the problem with me is, I don't want to leave you alone. The more time I spend with you, the more I want to see you."

He squeezes my hand tightly, almost painfully. I wince. He lets go and mutters an apology. Then he shoves his hands in his pockets and dips his chin to his chest.

"What's wrong? Did I say too much?"

He shakes his head, then looks up with a grimace. His eyebrows furrow so tightly together, they become a unibrow. "No, no. It's music to my ears. But I have to tell you something about me and Daisy."

My stomach drops and I step back. People walk between us. I can't believe it. I'm going to be sick. "Oh my God! You're—You're together?" There's venom in my voice, but he laughs. *Laughs!* "It's not fucking funny."

"She's my sister."

Relief tries to creep in, but anger does too. Why is this such a secret?

"And my last name isn't Ariti."

My mouth drops open and I try to speak. "What? What do you mean?"

"That's my mother's maiden name. Can we please go somewhere else to talk so I can explain?"

I cross my arms and stay right where I am. "No. Explain now."

"Well, then we have a problem. I don't talk about my private life out in the open. Of all people, you should remember that. That's why I use Ariti." His voice is firm but hushed. He's not going to budge.

I'm in a battle with myself. All I'm used to are lies. That's a road I said I wouldn't go down again. I let him kiss me enough to make me want to sleep with him, but if we're at this point, why hasn't he—or at least Daisy— told me this already? If they had, I wouldn't have been worried that they might have that kind of history together. They don't really share a physical resemblance. My frustration is building.

A cackle escapes my lips. "No wonder you want to talk about me all the time. Here I was, thinking a guy actually wanted to get to know me, but no. You were just distracting me from asking you questions. Great way to start a relationship... if you can even call this that," I snap. "Honesty is already out of the fucking window."

"Are you finished?" *Oh, really!* "I know I should've told you. I'm sorry. I just wanted to enjoy the time I had with you… Wanted to forget who I was for a little while. Why is that so horrible?"

With my chin raised, I don't answer.

"I never tell people more than they need to know about me. It's for a good reason. It's to protect me and Daisy from an invasion of privacy. Especially now that my photography has become more popular. I hardly know you, why would I dump all my baggage on you? And believe me, you don't want to know all that anyway."

A little voice whispers he might be right, but I ignore it. "Don't you think I should be the judge of that?" I move closer to him again, but only because this zigzagging between people is annoying. So is this entire situation.

"No. Not yet. I've kept my mouth shut my entire life. Why would you expect me to tell you everything about me after a couple of weeks… not even a couple of weeks? Just telling you I'm color-blind was hard enough. And please don't tell anyone that, by the way. I don't get involved with women because of this, but I thought you were different and would understand. All I'm asking is that you be patient with me."

"I don't know what to say to that. I'm an open book. What you see with me is what you get. And when I look at you, I see someone who I could fall for. I'm not talking about the photographer. Just a handsome man who makes me feel more special than anyone I've known. Now, all I see is an act."

His large hands embrace my shoulders and give them a gentle squeeze. "It wasn't. I swear to you. I'm happy and full of hope when I'm around you. Those are things I never thought were possible, at least not at this point in my life. I didn't think this was in the cards for me. Please understand."

I shake his hands off me and step back. "You might think it's not a big deal, but I do. I gotta go. I can't think when you're nearby." Before he can respond, I walk away.

His voice blows words into the wind behind me, but I escape before they can catch me and I give in.

I don't want to hear him.

But my heart says I should.

Staples is my favorite store right now. I just got back to the gallery after buying another huge container of rubber bands—well, two. One for my apartment and another to stash in my office. I toss them on my desk. I paced back and forth all night last night, yanking on those stupid things. I broke most of them. A couple of them hit me in the face when I lost control. One just missed my eye. I need a healthier way to release tension, maybe kickboxing or something.

I'm assuming Julius's last name is Levi, since that's Daisy's. But what if hers is fake too? Are they ex-cons or something? *Grr.* I know I'm being extreme. His face turned to marble last night, but the softness in his eyes stayed. Or sadness.

Look at how he is with Chance. *Everybody deserves a chance no matter how broken they are.* That phrase is playing on a continual loop in my head. The more I think about it, the more I think Julius might be as broken as Chance, and maybe Daisy is too. What the hell happened to them that they go through so much to keep it behind them?

Every time my phone pinged today, I looked at it, hoping it was a message from him. Finally I realized how stupid that was—he doesn't have my number. He could get it if he wanted it, but it's probably easier to close himself off instead.

And at this point, I wouldn't even know what to say.

The buzzer rings, alerting me someone's entered the gallery. I check my appearance in the mirror and just shrug my shoulders. Despite only a few good hours of sleep last night, I don't look too bad. I step into the showroom to find Daisy at the front desk.

"Hi, Daisy." *Keep it casual.* "I was just about to send you the numbers for this week."

"Let's not pretend I'm here for business reasons. Just give me a few minutes of your time, then I'll leave you alone."

I nod. "Do you want to sit down?"

"Actually, no. I can't stay long." She folds her hands in front of her.

"So what's up?"

"This is a unique situation that Julius and I are in with you. Business has always been business. Cut and dry. Then you came along and added a new dynamic. I'm still trying to get a grip on it myself because of the change in Julius. Well, up until last night, when he came home even more miserable than before he met you."

"So it's my fault?"

"That's not what I'm saying. He… we're sorry we didn't tell you he uses a pseudonym, but why should we have when at first it was just business? You knew Julius was complicated before you met him. There's obviously a reason he's the way he is. The way I am. Look at me." She points to her body. "I'm covered in tattoos. Do you think I do it for fun?"

I shake my head. For some reason I feel tears forming.

"You're damn right, no. It's my way of hiding. Most people have secrets to hide, some bigger or smaller than others, but we hide them in our own ways to protect ourselves."

Dear God, what happened to them?

"Why are you here? Why are *you* telling me this and not Julius?"

She braces herself on the edge of the desk with her hands. "I'm doing this for him because he has always taken care of me. It's my turn to take care of him. Meeting you put a crack in his wall. You've opened his eyes. No one, and I mean no one, has ever been able to do that before. To hear him talk about a woman the way he talks about you has convinced me that you're special. Even Chance thinks you're special. Maybe you're exactly who Julius needs to pull him from the darkness.

He might not be able to see color, but he seems to see your light."

"So what are you asking of me?" I sit on the edge of the desk.

"Just give the man some time. Don't walk away from him when you don't know the full story yet. I know it won't be easy, but it's not impossible either. We can go back to doing business if you want and pretend this never happened. But it'd be a pity. Because he really likes you. And I like you too."

That makes me crack a smile. "Thanks, Daisy. But you know, this isn't easy for me either. I really like your brother… and it's weird for me to say that. I had begun to think maybe you two were together. You were obviously more than just agent and artist."

Daisy covers her mouth like she's going to puke.

"Yeah," I say. "My thoughts exactly." We chuckle. "I have my own horrible history with relationships. I've been lied to, used, cheated on… This feels like a repeat in the works. You have to know where I'm coming from."

"In a way I do, but this isn't about me. It's about you and Julius. I'm not going to try to influence you, and I know it won't be easy. Only you know what your heart is saying. Follow your instincts." She pulls a piece of paper out of her bag and places it on the front desk. "Here's our address." My eyes pop open. "Yes, we live together."

I glance at it. "Why are you giving me this? And is it safe to assume I should ask for Julius Levi? That was never confirmed the other night."

"Yes, it's Levi. I'm going away for the weekend. I'm

leaving tomorrow morning and won't be home until late Sunday night. He'll be home alone. Well, except for Chance, of course. I'll leave your name at the security desk so they'll let you up to our penthouse." *Penthouse?* "I think it's what you both need. No interruptions. Try it one more time."

"I can't promise anything."

"I'm not asking you to."

16

JULIUS

Since when have I had a problem with silence? *Never.* Until Sky came along. The one I thought would change everything. The light I was never expecting… and now it's dark again. I could watch her all day long and snap a million pictures. Yes, I know that sounds creepy. But sitting with her at dinner two nights ago was entertaining and gave me a glimpse into who she really is. She talks a lot but not in an annoying way. Intelligence pours from her beautiful mouth. Her background in the arts is amazing.

She has a patchwork family that seems to work well together, and I find myself jealous. In my life, it's just me and Daisy. No family barbecues to go to or big Thanksgiving or Christmas celebrations. No one to kiss when the ball drops on New Year's Eve, no friends to travel with, no kids. I live a lonely life. I have Daisy, but she's gathered a group of friends who are a good influence on her. She's not dependent on me anymore.

Just being with Skylar a few times has shown me how truly alone I am.

Why don't Daisy and I travel? I don't know. She has more friends than I do. She could travel with them, but she doesn't. Why don't we take advantage of the money we make? What are we saving it for? Maybe because we had nothing when we grew up, and deep down we're afraid that it could happen again.

There's no guarantee I'll be a successful photographer forever. Just the thought gives me the chills. Photography is my life. How would I live without it?

The doorbell rings, and my shoulders droop. I'm sure it's Candy from down the hall again. I want to ignore whoever's there, but I need to move my legs anyway. The doorbell rings again, and my stomach growls. I place my new camera on the living room table and make a mental note to order takeout.

"I'm coming," I growl. Chance beats me to the door and sniffs. Then he goes ballistic. My heart rate spikes when I look through the peephole. How did she get up here? I open the door immediately, my hand around Chance's collar.

"Sky! Umm, hi." Idiot. That rhymed.

Silence ensues, even though Chance is doing everything in his power to jump on her. Warmth gathers within me. Her eyes smolder as they trace my body, then come back to focus on my chest. I glance down and realize I'm wearing only a pair of old jeans. No shirt. I clear my throat and catch her attention.

"Hi, Julius. I'm sorry I've come unannounced." She cracks a smile when she glances at Chance. He whines desperately. Her smile grows. The desire to kiss those dazzling lips is almost beyond my control.

I clear my throat and step to the side. "Come in."

She walks through the door and I close it. I release my grip on Chance's collar, and he's on her in seconds.

She sits on the floor right there in the entryway, hugging and petting him. I'm not jealous.

"Someone's happy to see me," she coos. "I knew at least one of you would be, so I brought you a present. Now you have to sit for me. Can you do that?" He sits proud, then offers his paw without her asking. She looks up at me and nods. "You've trained him well."

She shuffles through her bag and pulls out a big squeaky bone. She squeezes it a few times, then offers it to him. "Here you go. Now you can annoy your dad with this noise all the time." He takes it and lies on the floor, chewing away, firing off squeaks every two seconds.

"I'm not sure I'm going to be thankful for that toy if it becomes his favorite," I grouse. Then I reach out my hand to help her up. She takes hold of it, and her smile becomes contagious. Once she's up, she doesn't let my hand go right away. Her eyes shine bright, making me believe that things might work out between us.

She lets go of my hand and looks around cautiously. "Is this a bad time? I don't want to interrupt anything." I have to force myself not to grab her and kiss her senseless.

"Other than the ladies hiding in the other room, I'm alone," I say, unable to hide the humor in my voice.

She arches an eyebrow. "I see you're in a playful

mood."

"I wasn't until a few minutes ago. Actually, I was more lost in a bad one." I raise my arm and motion for her to head into the living room. I force my eyes to look ahead instead of at how her ass fills out her pants. I've never been an ass guy before, but she's changing everything about me.

She twirls around in the middle of the open space. "Look at this place. It's beautiful." She walks over to the ceiling to floor windows and glances outside. "Great view."

"Thanks. I hope you don't have a fear of heights."

"Nope," she says, then turns around and continues to scope out the place. "It's a great size for you and Daisy."

"Wait... How did you know Daisy lives here?"

"How do you think I got up here unannounced?" She tosses an evil smirk over her shoulder. "Yep. Just as I thought—mostly black, white, and gray. Clean and crisp. Not too fancy."

I shrug. "That's my life. I need it a little darker in here... because of my light sensitivity. Daisy adds color with little accents throughout the place. You should see her bedroom and office. We're just happy to have a roof over our heads; we don't really care how this place is decorated."

"Oh, don't get me wrong. There's actually a warm feeling to it. I like it." She plops down on the gray sectional and rests her head back, arms sprawled out to the sides. "This is the most comfortable couch. Mine is old and the cushions are all deformed."

"Do you want a tour?" I ask. She hops off the couch, but then her gaze roams over my chest again. I need to get a T-shirt! I like how she's drinking me in, though.

After a few seconds, her eyes make their way to my face and she replies, "Yes. I'd love that."

"Okay. So you see where the kitchen is." I motion to the left of the living room. She nods.

"Nice. So much cabinet space. Sparkling clean too. At least from this distance."

"Let's go down the hall here to the right. This is where our bedrooms, bathrooms, and exercise room is." I let her go ahead of me and watch as she peeks her head into each door, not going into the rooms, though.

"It's amazing how huge this place is."

"I'm not done showing you the rest."

Her eyes spring open. "There's more?"

I nod. "Follow me." I lead her to the other side of the penthouse to a door. "This was a big reason we decided on this place. The person who lived here before us ran their business from home. This door joins us to an integrated office space next door. Daisy and I have our own offices, and my studio is in there too. This way, Daisy and I can keep our personal life separated from business. There's outside access too, so clients never enter our home." We stand in front of the conjoining door.

"Come on. Open the door. I want to see what it looks like. I'll be shocked if it's just as big as this part."

"Don't get too excited. It's not much different than here. Decoration wise."

"I don't care. Just do it." She bumps me with her hip.

I usher her through the door and into an open space much like our living room but smaller. "This area is used for breaks or just for the models or other clients to relax when they're waiting for me or Daisy. There's the small kitchen to the left and a bathroom by the front door. Let me take you to my office—whatever I need it to be. It's the first door on the right." I motion for her to go ahead of me.

She opens the door, walks in, and gasps.

"What's the matter?"

She shakes her head. "Nothing. I'm just amazed at the number of cameras on your desk... and the wall-to-wall photos."

"I was cleaning lenses earlier today. It's my favorite hobby when my mind is somewhere else. This room is my hall of fame. I prefer to display these in one place, not hanging everywhere."

She walks along one wall of photographs. I can't believe she's here right now.

"Oh, I love this one," she gushes and steps closer to the photo. "I don't want to know how you got a body—or is that hair?—to look like a tree."

I step into the room and turn around. "I tried to replicate this."

"Omigosh! Wow, that's gorgeous!" She walks up behind me and stops. Silence. Just when I can't take it a single second longer, her soft finger outlines the branches of the black tree tattoo that covers my entire back. "Mmm, I thought I saw a splash of ink near your upper shoulder, maybe your neck, the first day we met. This is so amazing. Does it have a special meaning?"

I glance over my shoulder at her. "It does, but you'll think it's stupid."

"Try me."

"The tree of life. Some believe it represents new beginnings, bright futures, positivity. When we moved to New York City, Daisy and me, our entire world became better. We finally had a future to look forward to. Sure, my past was weighing me down, but somehow, I knew I was going to do whatever it took to be a successful photographer. I was just a teenager, but I knew, regardless of my issues, I'd get there."

Her finger stops on one spot. I know exactly what it is. "Why is there a broken branch?"

"Some say a broken branch is the death of a relationship. That one has a double meaning for me. Maybe one day I'll tell you about it." I turn around to find her eyes pleading with me to share something—anything—more about my past.

Then she reaches out to touch my arm. "Just know, if you do ever want to confide in me, I'll never tell another soul."

I cup her soft cheeks with my hands and gently kiss her lips. She places one of her hands over mine. "I promise," she murmurs, holding my gaze so the truth sinks in.

"Thank you." I let my forehead rest against hers. "That means more than you can know."

Squeak. Chance interrupts us as he walks into the office, and we split apart. Skylar pats his side. I gently remind him that he's not allowed in my office. There are simply too many things he could damage. He goes back out and plops down on the hallway floor in front of the office, squeaking away.

"So… do you use the same tattoo artist as Daisy?" She's behind me again. "This tree is a work of art. The detail that went into it is terrific. How long did it take to complete it?"

"Almost two years."

"Wow. That's crazy," she comments, walking around me, then continues to check out the rest of the pictures. "Why is this camera in a display case? It looks pretty beat up." She leans over the case to see it better.

"That's my very first camera. My mom gave it to me when I turned thirteen."

Skylar turns around and folds her hands in front of her, giving me her full attention as always.

"She spent most of her tip money to buy that for me. It was the most expensive gift I'd ever received. I asked her why she gave me a camera of all things; I hadn't asked for one and I wasn't even sure I could use it with my eyesight. She said it was good for black and white photos, and she wanted a glimpse of how I see the world. When things got rough at home, she'd tell me and Daisy to go outside and take pictures, to go get lost in another world for a little while. That camera changed my life, maybe even saved me." I walk over to the case and point to a picture hanging on the wall above it. Skylar turns around and stands next to me. "See this picture of a butterfly?"

"It's color," she says, surprise in her voice. "I can't

believe I didn't notice it right away."

"It's one of the first photos I took. My first roll of film was color. After that, she bought me black and white film. This is the only color photo I kept. I took it for my mom. I told you how she loved butterflies. She had it developed and framed. Somehow, it's survived all these years."

Skylar glances at me and strokes my arm with her soft hand. "Thank you for telling me these things about you. It helps me understand you a bit more, but it also makes me more curious. That's not fair." The mood gets lighter in the room.

"Come on. Let's finish the tour of this place." We go out to the hallway, and I lead her to my studio.

She steps in and looks around. "This is great! Another huge room. No wonder you use it for a studio. Look at all the lights, tripods, and other gadgets. Great sheepskin rug. I've never seen one so big." She kneels down and brushes her hand over it. "It's so soft," she gushes. A funny expression crosses her face and she suddenly pulls her hand away. "But... I don't want to know how many naked women have been on there. Or in this room, as a matter of fact."

"Actually, no one has. It's brand new. I just got it and wanted to air it out. I'm hoping to use it for my next project, if it ever materializes."

"Good answer." She stands back up and wanders through the room, careful not to touch anything. Other than equipment, there isn't much to see here.

I remain by the door and lean against the frame. When she's finished looking around, she walks toward me. We stare at each other in silence for a long moment. The room becomes increasingly warm.

"Tell me why you're here, Sky."

She pushes her hair away from her face and takes a deep breath. "I didn't like how the other night ended. The last few days, I've been in a funk, trying to see both sides of the story. Not that I know much of your story or anything, but you know what I mean. Why I was annoyed; why you need to be secretive. I'll admit it, I have major trust issues when it comes to men and that's why I got pissed. I'm always the last one to know something. I refuse to be that woman again.

"Then you came along and... and you have trust issues too. But I didn't understand why Daisy being your sister was such a big deal. Why not just tell me that from the second you knew who I was? Especially since I work with both of you. And your last name? Yes, we're kind of strangers too, but we have a connection. And then, when we... well, you know..." She stops, her frustration obvious. "You know what I mean, don't you?" *Yes.* She pulls on her hair. "Ugh. Why is this so damn hard?"

Help her out! "Because we're both kind of clueless as to what's going on between us? I've been doing a lot of thinking too, mostly about you. Hoping that we weren't over when we'd only just begun. When I think too much, I buy more equipment that I probably don't need. Incidentally, did I show you my new camera? I'm blaming it and this rug on you," I tease.

"Haha." She inches even closer. "Did you come to a conclusion about me? About us?"

I nod. "I don't want to walk away and go back to

living in my hole. I've felt more alive during the short amount of time I've spent with you than I ever have before. Regardless of my success in my career. This is a completely different feeling. You have to understand, this is totally new for me." I rake my hands through my hair. "Yeah, I've been on dates, but I've never been in a serious relationship before. Those women didn't mean anything to me compared to how I feel about you. As you can guess, expressing myself isn't my specialty."

"Hmm. You could've fooled me. I love the way you talk about us. But I know another way for you to express yourself." She places her hands on my chest, reminding me again that I'm shirtless. She doesn't seem to mind… her soft fingers trace my skin, releasing waves of heat in their wake. "You said you wanted me in front of your camera, and I'd love to see you in action. Photograph me. Not just my face. Show me how you see me through your eyes."

What?! That's not what I expected to hear.

I wrap my hands around hers and press my lips to them. "Are you sure? There's no pressure. We have time. It doesn't have to be tonight."

She squeezes my hands in return. "I'm positive. But let's do this quick, before I chicken out."

"I'd be honored." I look at her, then glance at the rug behind her. "I have an idea." Her eyes flash, and I worry that she'll change her mind. I try to reassure her. "Hear me out first, then let me know if it's okay."

"Sure. Tell me. I trust you."

Music to my ears.

But why does it scare the shit out of me?

17

SKYLAR

When I arrived and he opened the front door, I knew I was his. My heart fluttered like butterfly wings, and everything inside me lit up. And all that just from seeing his heart-stopping smile. He was dressed exactly the way I'd envisioned him in that fantasy the other day. His chiseled abs, hard pecs, and solid biceps made it almost impossible for me not to touch him. I'm proud of myself—I don't think he noticed how tempted I was. Well, I did have to force my gaze to stay up top... Thankfully, Chance was there, as usual, to distract me.

Julius's tattoo is magical. Who would think to put a huge tree tattoo on their back? I like that it's black. I don't like colorful tattoos on men anyway, but his explanation of why he chose the tree gave me a glimpse of his past. And the broken branch is so full of underlying meaning. Death of a relationship. He made it sound like his mom died. Does it represent her? Or did they have a bad relationship and he walked away... But then there was the story about that first camera.

Trees represent a fresh start and positivity. He seems to have taken advantage with his success, but he's still fighting demons. I haven't seen any real positivity. What's holding him back? Daisy gives off more of an optimistic vibe. Man, he's hard to understand.

And then he explained his idea… and here I am.

Julius returns to the studio and hands me a fluffy white robe. "Here you go," he says. I brush my hand over it and can't wait to snuggle up in it. It's soft like kitten fur. I wonder if I can take it home. "Let me show you where the bathroom is."

He leads the way, and I'm happy because I can admire his tattoo even more. His back is broad at the top and gradually tapers down to a slick V.

Squeak.

I glance back to see Chance following us, the toy I brought in his mouth. I swear, I love this dog. You can't not be happy with him around. I certainly know why Julius loves him so much.

"Here you go." Julius opens a door near the waiting area. I walk in and turn around to face him. He puts his hands on my shoulders. "Only down to what you're comfortable with. I'll be waiting in the studio." His warm lips brush my forehead, and my pulse quickens with pleasure. I close my eyes and revel in his earthy, male scent.

"Gotcha. Just give me a few minutes. Are you sure you want me to wash my face? I don't need any makeup?"

"Nope. Even though you don't wear a lot, I want you as natural as possible. Keep the toe ring and any other jewelry." He touches the diamond stud in my nose lightly.

I eye him curiously. "Hmm. Things have just gotten more interesting."

"Hey! Who's the photographer here?"

"You. Blah, blah, blah…"

He laughs. "Just do as I say. I promise you won't regret it. There are fresh towels under the sink."

"Okay, okay." I step back to close the door, but Chance tries to weasel his way in. Julius stops him.

"No, Chance. I know you're just as curious as I am, but no." I laugh, and he smirks at me.

"See you in a few." I close the door and lean against the back of it.

Am I really going to do this? I'm still surprised that I asked him to take pictures of me. I don't regret it, but I am questioning it now because I'm chicken shit. His idea is a little wild. I made him promise he won't show anybody the photos. Not even Daisy. It's too private for me. He's not pushing—he says I only need to take off as much as I'm comfortable with. But I'm not a model who doesn't care how much skin is showing.

I inhale deeply. *Okay. You can do this!*

My heart is pounding. I wrap the robe tightly around me and exit the bathroom. My heart melts when I see Chance all curled up in a little bed sleeping, his new bone tucked under his chin. I was wondering if he'd be prancing around while Julius took the pictures. It would've been kind of awkward.

The hardwood floor of the studio feels cool against my feet. The AC is blasting, but I don't think I'll be cooled off any time soon. Julius is busy positioning a spotlight near the rug. His back is toward me and I don't think he's heard me. He's still shirtless, which I love. How am I going to control myself when he's half-naked and I'll be fully naked with just a white sheet wrapped around me?

I suddenly need a drink with a lot of alcohol in it. Should I ask for one? *No, Skylar! Confidence is all you need!*

"Hey. I'm ready when you are." I bob back and forth on my heels.

"Give me a second. This light doesn't want to cooperate. Usually my assistants take care of this stuff." He steps back and looks it over. "That'll work." He glances my way, then stands up straight. I shove my restless hands into the pockets of the robe. "Mmm. Perfect."

I ruffle my hair. "You sure? Is my hair okay?"

He lifts his hand in my direction. "Stop! Don't touch it. I want it… I want you just the way you are right now. Are you sure you're ready?"

I nod. It's now or never.

"Great. Here's the satin sheet. I'll show you what I need you to do, then I'll leave you to get into position. When you're ready, just yell my name."

I'd rather be yelling your name for another reason.

He explains how I should wrap the white sheet around my body, covering only the intimate parts. I think he wants to help me, but he's afraid to touch me.

Keeping this session professional won't be easy for either of us. And he doesn't even know yet that I've decided to go naked under the sheet. Where this boldness is coming from is beyond me. I mean, I'm pretty confident most of the time, but this situation has broken down all my barriers. And I'm as vulnerable as I feel.

He leaves the room and I follow his instructions. It takes a few times to get situated the way he described in the middle of the sheepskin rug. Finally, I've got the sheet wrapped around my chest and my lower abdomen, coming up from behind. It covers a bit of my hip while revealing most of my upper thigh and the rest of my leg. Then it goes between my legs, just covering my private area. I feel very sexy and Greek goddess-like, but I should probably wait until I see the pictures before I say that aloud.

I find a comfortable position and prop my head on my right hand. I spread my left hand out on the rug in front of me for support. "Julius, I'm ready," I call. My heart pounds in my throat. I realize I can't see the doorway.

The doorknob jiggles, then I hear the door open and close. The sound of his bare feet on the floor resonates within the fairly empty room. Silence. I look up to find him staring at me. His eyes are practically black, and his jaw is clenched. I want to tell him I know how he feels because this is probably the most sexual thing I've ever done… and it isn't meant to be. Or is it? But knowing that I'm naked under this sheet is such a turn-on for me.

His sizzling gaze practically burns my skin. "You looked perfect in a simple robe, but you look even better wrapped up in a sheet. Just to let you know, normally I don't take pictures of faces, only bodies. This time I'd like to take pictures of your face too. Is that okay with you?"

"Yes, but I'm going to be clear. These pictures are for us, and nobody else is allowed to see them. If they're just of my face, I don't care. Anything else is for our eyes only."

"I promise. I don't want to share," he says firmly.

"You don't want to share the photos… or *me*?" I say with a sultry voice, pushing my hair over my shoulder so it exposes my neck.

18

JULIUS

My gaze wanders over her voluptuous body as I drink her in. She appears to be naked under the sheet. *Really?* I'm both surprised and thrilled. There's no hint of underwear peeking out and her pebbled nipples don't try to hide. I don't know how I'm going to manage to control myself and keep my head on straight. My restraint is ready to snap like one of her rubber bands.

"You are one of a kind, Sky. Sharing is out of the question." She's never told me she's mine, but I can't help but feel possessive of her. I just found her. I'll be damned if someone takes her away from me.

"Good answer," she purrs. "I don't like to share either." She flashes me a sexy smile, then lowers her head and rests it on her outstretched arm. Simply perfect. *I'm a dead man.*

I bought this rug for her, to do this exact thing. I didn't know if I'd ever get to speak to her again, but I was hoping I was wrong. I've never felt such need or want toward a woman… ever.

Time for business. "Sky, don't move. That's the perfect position to start with. Let me check the lighting, and we'll begin. The light throws off heat, so hopefully the room will warm up for you."

"I'm fine—getting warmer by the minute, just watching you."

I take a deep breath and try not to react to her loaded comment. I adjust a couple of things then click the shutter several times. I review the camera display. "Okay, perfect. Now drape your left leg in front of the right." She follows. "Good. Pull your knee up toward your belly just a tad."

"Like this?"

"Not quite. May I touch your leg?"

"Sure. You know what you want."

I do indeed. I kneel down and reach out to her. My hand connects with her silky skin, and I have to swallow down a moan. This is going to be the biggest test of my life.

Goosebumps form on her skin. "You're cold."

She releases a tiny laugh. "The goosebumps aren't because of that. A certain sexy photographer just touched my thigh and made me shiver. I must be sensitive." She props her head on her hand. Her other hand caresses up my thigh. I stand up quickly because my body's on high alert. Keep this up, and I won't need a tripod to hold my camera.

"You know what? You're dangerous. That's what I'm going to call you from now on." Dangerous because she's changing my life. How can one person make every-thing more exciting and better? "You're making it very hard to stay professional... Don't move." *Click.*

"You're not so innocent yourself. I had a fantasy. Curious what it was?"

"One second... Can you lie on your back for me?" She complies. I stand over her so she's between my legs. "Put your left arm under your head. Okay, now angle your head to the right so I can get your sexy nose ring thing in the picture. Smile slightly but don't show your teeth. Look forward, not at me." She follows my direc-tion and nails it. "Are you sure you've never modeled before?"

"Only for you. You're hard to say no to. Can I tell you my fantasy yet?

"No. I need to focus. Let's finish this first." She pouts and I can't prevent the grin forming on my face behind the camera.

Time flies by, and I enjoy every minute of it. I could spend the entire night here, but I remind myself that she came to see me, not the camera. I'm about ready to toss the thing and rip that sheet off her.

I stop and observe her. "Who are you? The Sky I know just told me a little while ago that she's never modeled before. But you— You let your walls down and really played the role. You're amazing."

Looking high on life, she turns on her side and props her head up again, just like she was when we started. Sexy as sin. "You're the reason," she confesses. "You make me feel like I'm the most attractive woman in the world. It was just you and me in this room having fun.

I've never felt so confident in my body." She crooks her finger, calling me in. Her eyes sparkle with mischief. "Lose the camera."

I raise my eyebrows in wonderment, then set the camera swiftly down on the table and turn the spotlight off. I get down on my knees and crawl over to her like I'm stalking my prey. The vision of her in front of me is something I won't need a picture of. It will be locked in my mind forever as one of the best experiences of my life.

If I don't kiss her soon, I'm going to lose my fucking mind.

As I inch closer, she puts up her hand for me to stop. "Just to make sure… this shoot has officially ended right? You're no longer Julius Ariti?"

"Nope. I kicked his ass out the door once the last picture was taken. He knows you're mine now. He doesn't get to see this." The corner of her mouth quirks up.

"See what?" She rolls onto her back and drops her arms to her sides. I move over her, hovering with my hands next to her head and my knees caging her in. I don't let my body touch hers yet.

Her fiery gaze roams my face and stops on my lips. I lick the top one and her eyes flash. Her mouth opens slightly, and I lower my head so our lips are almost touching.

"Julius," she mumbles. "Don't make me be——"

My mouth captures hers before she can finish, and my senses go into overdrive just from the taste of her.

She sucks on my lower lip, then nips it hungrily. "Can I tell you my fantasy now? Actually there are two."

"Hurry," I urge as I line needy kisses along her jaw and then down her slender throat.

"The first time I met you, even though you were an arrogant jerk, I pictured you as a fireman coming out of a burning house. You only had pants with suspenders on, muscles tight and slick, with a hose hanging over your shoulder." She rakes her nails gently up and down my back. Now I'm the one with goosebumps.

"Are you done?"

"Nope."

I drop my head into the crook of her neck and take a deep breath. She continues.

"I've dreamed of you circling around me, just waiting to pounce. I was naked and couldn't move... At your mercy. Does that sound tempting?" she murmurs into my ear with heated breaths.

I lower my mouth to her heaving chest. My tongue sweeps over her full breasts right above the edge of the sheet. Her nails dig into my back and I release a groan. My body flushes with heatwaves.

"Last one." Her breathing quickens. "I also imagined you just like you are now. Shirtless, low-hanging jeans, and disheveled hair. But you're better than any fantasy."

"No more talking," I mumble, my lips rendering her speechless.

19

SKYLAR

His mouth is devouring mine, making my head spin. Finally, his hands start to roam my body. Gently, like he's afraid to hurt me, but it's enough to drive me freaking crazy. And all the while, he's still hovering over me. I want his hard body flush against mine, but this damn sheet and his sexy jeans are preventing that from happening.

I tear my mouth away, missing his lips already. He looks at me with questioning eyes.

"I want your warm skin against mine," I murmur, brushing my finger along his jawline. "Want to help me get out of this sheet?"

His eyes darken and his tight jaw ticks. He pushes off the floor, then maneuvers himself so he's upright on his knees next to me. I raise my arms above my head, and arch my back. He finds the end of the sheet underneath and tugs gently.

Julius glances at my covered breasts, then at me.

"Sky." My name drips off his lips like honey, and I fall for him even more. "Are you sure?"

He's going to strip me bare, and I realize this is both a physical and emotional act. I trust him wholeheartedly —and it's a completely new sensation for me.

"Julius, I want this... I want you... more than anyone."

And with one fell swoop, my chest is bare. The air is cool against my nipples, then he captures one in his warm, hungry mouth. I release a cry of pleasure, running my fingers through his hair, encouraging him to keep going. He nuzzles my sensitive breasts, then kisses upward till he reaches my mouth. I open up for him and seek his tongue greedily.

Suddenly he breaks the kiss and flashes me a devilish smirk. "There's still more of you to discover."

"You're going to torture me, aren't you?" I grasp the rug beneath me to control myself. My heart's ready to jump out of my chest.

"I think you want me to," he says playfully.

I moan in delight when his finger traces down the side of my left breast. His soft, needy lips tease the exposed skin along the way until he reaches another curve of the sheet around my hip.

I lift my hips so he can set the fabric free, leaving only my core covered. He slowly massages up my inner thigh to the remaining end of the loose sheet. He grips it in his hands and looks deep into my eyes, asking me silently for permission for the last time.

"Yes," I whisper desperately. His eyes blaze with desire.

He tears the sheet away from me and tosses it to the side. My body quivers as a quick cool breeze filters over my skin. In seconds, our lips connect as I pull his slick, hard body onto mine. Our hands frantically explore each other, demanding more. When my fingers connect with his jeans, I fumble for the button to open them, but he pulls away and stands up quickly.

"It'll be a lot easier and faster if I do it this way."

I push up onto my elbows and watch with amazement. He's beautiful—tight abs, flexed biceps working open his jeans, that treasure trail pointing to what awaits inside. This confidence to lie here naked in front of him in a bright room is unfamiliar to me, but I love it. The anticipation is killing me as he slowly unbuttons his jeans and pushes down the zipper. My mouth goes dry.

"Commando," I observe. "Always full of surprises."

He huffs a laugh. "Just as surprised as I was to see you had nothing on under that sheet. I wanted to rip it off as soon as I walked in the room. And then you let me unwrap you like a Christmas present." The jeans are finally off, exposing his beautiful body. A delicious shudder pulses through me.

I pat the spot next to me on the rug. "Get down here, and let's see what other fantasies we can make come true."

"I like the view from up here. You're absolutely the sexiest woman I've ever met."

His feral eyes scan my body from head to toe. I feel the heat when they pause at various places and enjoy every second of his perusal. Finally, he gets down and stretches out on top of me, resting his weight between my legs, spreading them further apart. My body molds against his. Our eyes lock and we give ourselves to each other without saying another word. His mouth crashes onto mine and sparks of electricity shoot to my fingers and toes. I wrap my legs around his waist as he rubs sensuously against me. It's been so long that I'm ready to come undone already.

"I can't get enough of you," he whispers against my skin, inching down my body. An unashamed moan escapes me when his finger teases my most sensitive spot. "I want to go slow and savor everything, but I don't know how long I can last."

"Me neither." My body rubs against him at its own will.

"That's not helping. I can play that game too." He slides a finger inside me breathtakingly slow, and my back arches. My peaked nipples explode with heavenly sensations as they meet his chest.

"Ahh… that feels so good," I whimper between heated breaths. My hips move in sync with the teasing pace of his finger. "Do you have a condom?"

He stiffens. "Fuck! No! I haven't been with a woman in such a long time… Damn, Sky! If I knew this was how the evening was going to go, I would've been more prepared."

"Have you been tested recently? I have, and I'm clean… and I'm on the pill. I've been on a mission to stay away from men, so it's been a while," I mutter quickly.

He chuckles against my skin. "I *am* a man, if you haven't noticed."

"Oh, I have. You're just too hard to resist. Literally."
I squeeze his perfect ass. "Now please tell me you're
clean, because I saw something a lot bigger than your
finger a few minutes ago."

"Aren't you impatient! We have all night. But don't
worry—I'm clean. I promise." He teases me with two
fingers now.

I squeeze my eyes shut and shake my head back and
forth. "Oh, so good, but I need more." My nerve
endings will be fried by the end of this.

He pulls his hand away, then positions himself fully
between my quivering legs. I open my eyes when I feel
him at my core. His hooded gaze connects with mine as
he slides slowly into me, filling me completely. One or
both of us groan as he begins to move. I don't really
care because all I can focus on is how amazing he feels
inside me.

20

JULIUS

Her warmth that surrounds me is almost unbearable. The throaty sounds of pleasure escaping from deep within her urge me on. The moment we met, I knew my life would change, but I didn't expect anything like this. This is more than I could've dreamed of. Before her, I thought I had everything I needed. I didn't know she was missing, but here she is—the one I needed the most.

I turn us quickly so I'm on my back and she's on top of me. The vision of her rocking against me and her face reflecting complete bliss makes me almost go over the edge, but I want this to last.

"Julius, I'm close."

My hands stop her from moving. Her eyes spring open in surprise. I sit up and keep her in place so she's straddling me and we're face to face. "Not yet. Let me enjoy you just a little longer."

"Connected to you like this is beyond anything I could've imagined."

My mouth captures hers as I wrap my arms around her waist, pulling her flush against me. She wraps her arms around my shoulders, never breaking the kiss. My heart beats out of my chest and sweat trickles down my back. My hands travel down to her ass and we start to move in unison. Our kiss becomes so intense that I can hardly breathe, but I can't stop. She rocks harder against me, and I can feel we're close. I don't want to let go, but it's too intense.

She rips her lips from mine and the most beautiful sounds come out of her mouth as her body vibrates around me, taking me along with her. Flashes of light appear, and I swear I see color for the first time. Her colors.

We sit there, holding onto each other for dear life, as we slowly come down from our high. She relaxes her arms and leans back, then gazes at me like no other woman ever has. Like I'm her world. "Julius," she whispers.

I push her wild hair away from her face and kiss her swollen mouth. "I know. There are no words to describe this. It's like my life has just now begun." What Skylar and I just did was far beyond sex. I haven't been the same since I met her, my emotions and feelings are eternally changed. I hardly recognize myself when she's with me.

"Everything is happening so fast, but I can't slow it down. I don't want to because I'm already yours," she professes.

I close my eyes and drop little kisses above her heart.

She's either going to make me fall in love with her or she'll kill me with her words.

"You're the only woman who's ever said that to me. Thanks for taking a chance on me."

"Thanks for letting me. If it weren't for Chance knocking me over, maybe I wouldn't be here right now."

"Let's not think about it."

The door closes behind us. The smell of fresh pizza fills the air as the elevator rises to the top floor. When we finally came out of the studio for air, we realized we were starving. Chance's bladder was about to explode too, so we decided to take a quick walk and get pizza on the way home. And here we are.

"I don't think I'll ever look at a sheepskin rug the same way again. I'll probably blush every time," Skylar admits, then touches her cheeks. "See? I'm blushing right now."

What I wouldn't do to see what the blushing of her skin looks like. People say it's a rosy color. Well, I might not be able to see the color change, but I know her face should be warm. I lean in and kiss her cheek... or at least try to with two pizza boxes in my hand. Yup.

"I don't see it, but I can feel how warm your skin is."

Her hand cups her mouth. "Shit. I'm sorry. I wasn't thinking."

"It's no big deal. I'm used to it." I mumble in her ear, "I'm thinking more about the hot noises you made while on that rug and on me."

She swats my arm. "Oh, like you were quiet as a mouse. The neighbors were probably wondering what the hell you were doing."

The elevator comes to a stop and the door slides open. I wait while Chance and Skylar walk out first. "They knew full well what was going on, and they were jealous. The most beautiful woman rocked my world a couple times. I'm still coming down from the high."

"Am I the first one to christen that room? Or have you done that before? I'll be riddled with jealousy if you have, but I can't expect you not to have a past."

"You're the only one, and it'll stay that way."

She stops. I love the way her expression softens when she looks at me. We stand there with the boxes between us, then she leans over and I do the same. The taste of her lips is more delicious than any food. My body might be hungry, but it has enough energy for a couple more rounds.

There are voices in the distance. Someone is heading our way. We split apart. Coming toward us is Candy with a man I've never seen before. She's dressed nicely. Maybe it's a date. As we approach them, I find myself smiling at her.

Candy looks at me peculiarly. "Julius, is that you? I never thought I'd see the day you smiled at me." She's teasing, but I know she's being honest too. She glances at Skylar and her own smile spreads from ear to ear. "Oh, I see." She nods knowingly.

She introduces her date, and I introduce Skylar. I call her my girlfriend. I'm not sure if that's appropriate, but after tonight, things are on the fast track. We need to catch up to what we are.

Chance yanks on his leash. It's time for him to eat. We start to go our separate ways, but Candy stops. She turns back and addresses Skylar.

"Whatever you're doing, keep doing it. I've never seen Julius this happy." She laughs. "Actually, I've never seen him happy at all. He's practically glowing. And with the smile on your face and that sweet kiss over the pizza boxes we just saw… yeah." She pats Skylar on the arm and then does the same to me. "You two enjoy your pizza and *dessert*." I'm sure Skylar's blushing now. Maybe I am too.

We wave and watch them disappear down the hall. "Well, that was interesting," Skylar acknowledges when I open the door. Chance dashes inside, and I give the leash a tug.

"Chance, remember what I said. Ladies first." He barks, and I unhook the leash.

Skylar kicks off her shoes. "You guys are so adorable. Chance really understands you," she says. "He's one of a kind."

"So are you." I drop my shoes next to hers and pat her on the ass. "Ladies first." I motion for her to go ahead of me.

Once we're in the kitchen, I place the pizza boxes on the island.

"Where are the dishes?" she asks, reaching for a cabinet. I wrap my arm around her waist and turn her toward me. Our bodies press against the counter.

"You do make me smile a lot. Don't stop." I caress

her cheek with the back of my hand. Chance trots over and sits next to us as if what we're doing is fascinating.

"That's because we just had mind-blowing sex." She points to her upturned mouth. "I'm smiling like crazy too."

"That's true, and I hope we can do it again and again. I want to keep a smile on your face." I wiggle my eyebrows. "But you know what? Beyond sex, I like it when I'm around you. I'm glad you came over tonight."

Her slender fingers thread through the belt loops on my shorts. "Well, as long as we're open and honest with each other, I'll stick around and make sure you keep smiling too."

"Honesty's not a problem, openness will take some time."

"I know, I know. Can we eat now before I faint? I can hardly wait for a slice." She pecks my lips. "Again, where are your dishes?"

"The cabinet behind you. What do you want to drink?" I open the refrigerator and wait for her response.

"Do you have wine or beer?"

"No. Sorry. We don't keep alcohol in the house," I divulge.

"Okay. Water's fine. It's healthier anyway. But then again…" She crinkles her face. "Look at this greasy pizza. Oh, whatever. Who cares? We had a good work-out. Let's eat."

Chance gets fed and taken care of, then we sit across from each other at the island. She opens one of the boxes and drops some pizza on her plate.

"Can I ask you a question?" *Oh no. Here we go.* She folds her slice in half and lets the fat drip off onto the plate.

"It depends on what it is." I grab a slice and take a big bite so my mouth is full. Maybe I won't have to talk.

"Daisy mentioned that she doesn't drink alcohol, and you just said you don't keep any in the house. Is she a recovering alcoholic?" She munches on her slice.

Once my mouth is empty, I answer, "Sky, we're all fighting our own demons. Sadly, alcoholism was her way of fighting hers. I don't think she'd mind you knowing. She's well on her way to becoming a mentor soon. I'm really proud of how far she's come."

"Was she your agent at the time?" she asks, licking the tips of her fingers.

"It was right at the beginning. We weren't too involved yet. She hid her addiction well, but then things started to fall through—she'd forget things, come home late at night plastered. I didn't think much of it because I thought that's what young people do. But one morning, I found her downing vodka straight from the bottle and following it up with some orange juice." *Just like my father.* "That's when I knew."

She shakes her head. "That must've been horrible."

"I'm not going to lie, Sky. I've seen a lot of shit in my life that I wish I could unsee. But that? Yeah. She resisted for a while, but I finally got her into a good rehab. She's been sober ever since. I'm proud of her. But her story is for her to tell you, not me."

"She has a lot of butterfly tattoos. Is it because your mom likes them?"

"*Liked* them." Suddenly, I'm not hungry and I push my dish away from me. I pick up my napkin and twist it while I talk. "She died when we were teenagers."

"Oh, Julius. I'm so sorry. I didn't mean to pry."

"I know. Just trying to be open." She cocks an eyebrow, and I wink at her.

"Okay," she says. "Let me change the subject. How about your color blindness? Why don't you want anyone to know? It's nothing to be ashamed of."

"Well, it is when your whole childhood is spent hearing what a worthless freak you are. That you'll never make anything of yourself. I heard it every day from my drunk father until I was sixteen. When you hear it on repeat, you start to believe it. The kids in school bullied me relentlessly because of the sunglasses I had to wear and for other things. I know it's ridiculous now, but I just don't want people to know. I don't want sympathy, and I don't want it to seem like I'm using it to gain attention for my photographs."

"Look what you've accomplished. You could be an inspiration to others. Give others the hope and encouragement they desperately need to accomplish their dreams."

"I know what you mean, but what happened in my past should stay in the past. It's just like an author who uses a pen name—most of them don't want to be known either. They hide behind their aliases." I look down to find a pile of shredded napkins in front of me.

She wipes her mouth with a napkin. "How did you get through school? Didn't your teachers notice when you had to deal with colors or in art class or anything?"

"Oh, they knew. They gave me different assignments when necessary, but with a lot of help from them, I was able to attend school like anyone else. Don't get me wrong, it was hard as hell. College was more difficult. Someone who's color-blind probably shouldn't be in an arts program, but my experience, never-ending hard work, and will to never give up, got me through it. I'm still in contact with some of the college professors I had. They've contributed to my success. I was very fortunate. They gave me back the sense of self-worth my father worked so hard to destroy."

That's enough. I've said too much already.

"Wow, that's great you still talk to them."

"Yeah." I gather the napkin shreds into a ball and toss them on my plate. "It's annoying that I need help when shopping for clothes or anything colorful in general. Daisy always comes with me. I'll never be able to drive a car. It's not so bad in New York City, though. I don't need a car here."

"Are you from New York?"

"No. We grew up in Delaware. We moved here when Daisy was fourteen and I was sixteen." I'm being stupid. These are wide open answers that I know will initiate a lot of questions. I fiddle with the boxes on the island. "Are you finished with your pizza?" Chance sits near us and wags his tail. He's waiting patiently for some crusts to munch on.

"No." She puts out her hand to keep me from picking up the leftovers. "I'm still hungry. Something gave me a big appetite. Do you know what it was?" She bats her eyelashes.

And just like that, the mood switches to something happier. I've never told another person as much as I've already told her. What I like is that I didn't see pity all over her face. She just listened.

"Come here for a second," Skylar says with her signature smile. I walk over to her, hoping she won't ask any more questions. When I'm close enough, she grabs my shirt, pulls me close, and wraps her legs around me. "I can see it's not easy for you to open up. I told you before—everything you tell me will stay with me."

I lean over and kiss her lightly. "Thanks for not pushing."

"I want to see the smile you had when we walked through the door or when we christened that rug." She massages my face. "No more clenching of your jaw tonight unless it's because I've rocked your world again."

I chuckle. "I couldn't resist you even if I tried. You wouldn't be here if I could. Now finish your pizza."

I'm in the mood for dessert.

21

SKYLAR

I don't want to move or even open my eyes. The pillow I'm cuddling smells like Julius. We couldn't get enough of each other last night... or was it just a couple hours ago? So many unspoken words were communicated through our bodies. When I mentioned I should leave, he asked me to stay the night. I was caught off guard because this side of Julius still surprises me. He melts my heart when he kisses me or just holds my hand. We fell asleep in each other's arms. If someone told me he was like this the first time I met him, I would've laughed and walked away. But it's true. The prick on a stick has a heart of gold hidden under that tough exterior. I love it. I think I love him.

Something tickles my nose. I open my eyes to find Julius gazing down at me. "Mmm," I murmur. "Aren't I lucky to wake up naked in your bed and see your gorgeous face?"

He lies on his side, his head propped on his hand. "I could watch you sleep for hours. You had the cutest grin on your face, then I realized how much I like you in my bed, hugging one of my pillows, wrapped in my blankets."

"Aren't you the sweetest thing in the morning or whatever time it is. Couldn't sleep?"

"It's eight. I slept for a little while, but once I woke up, my mind wouldn't turn off." His smile dims.

My stomach turns, and I'm suddenly more awake. I tuck the pillow under my chest and brace myself on my elbows for whatever's coming. "What's the matter? Do you regret what happened?"

"No, no. Nothing like that. If anything, the opposite." He strokes my cheek, and I let my stiff arms and shoulders relax a little.

"Do you want to talk about it?" I inch closer to him, using the pillow to contain my boobs. They're ready to pop out and say good morning, but whatever's on his mind might not make me happy.

"I want to say no because that's what I always do. But our relationship has my head spinning. A couple of weeks ago, the only people I really interacted with were Daisy and Chance. Well, okay, he's an animal but whatever. My days were... flat. Same as my emotions. The only other thing that made me happy was my work. But you've barged into my world and spread your positive energy around me. I can't go back to what I was. After the opening, and having to talk to reporters and socialize, I thought I'd have run right back to where I'm safe."

"So what did you do?" It's like I'm reading an angsty book, hanging on the edge, wondering where he's going with this.

"I ran to you." *Oh.* Talk about a zap to the heart. "I kept finding myself at your gallery. Waiting to talk to you, to be near you."

Warmth spreads through my chest. I can't find the words to respond so I kiss him instead. Long and hard until he flips me under him so I'm on my back. He groans.

"You drive me crazy, Sky. My body is already alert, even after our marathon last night. But I need to get this off my chest because I might chicken out later." He grabs the blanket and covers me, then snuggles close. I like cuddling with him.

"So keep going. I want to know everything before you clam up."

He traces my lower lip with his finger, then his feather-soft lips follow.

"Stop that. You're distracting me," I tease.

"I want you, Sky." His sweet honesty lights me up… but he's not finished. "And it scares the shit out of me. I don't have a clue how to do this. I don't want to screw this up or to hurt you."

"We're both taking chances, Julius. I've been burned really bad in the past, and I've become leery of relationships. Don't you remember me saying I wanted to stay away from men? But after last night, I can't and won't stay away from you. I know you have a history, but it doesn't make me want to walk away." I caress the arm that's draped over me.

He still looks worried. "That's my point. If we want to take this to another level, I have to tell you everything.

You need to know before you decide whether you want to be with me or not."

I can't think of anything he could tell me right now that'll make me run.

"I'm listening. Don't hold back."

He closes his eyes as if he's giving himself a pep talk. I stroke his cheek. "Take a deep breath. I think once you get it out, you'll feel better."

"This won't be easy, so bear with me. I haven't spoken about it in a long time. Not even with Daisy." The anguish painted on his face is enough for me to already feel defensive for him.

"My father was a drunk bastard. He jumped from one job to the next because of his drinking. My mom worked her ass off to keep food on the table for us and to pay the bills. My father was mentally and physically abusive. He slapped my mom around in front of us. I remember every single time. As a little boy, I couldn't protect her. When I tried, he came after me with his belt. In some ways, I was glad because he focused on me, instead of Mom and Daisy, but—"

My body tenses with rage and I want to kick his father's ass. I try to stay calm but my heart pounds. No one deserves that. I always had a loving mom and a happy household. To urge him to keep going, I stroke his back.

"As time went by, Mom became very depressed. There were times when she'd just lie in bed, for days. She'd only come out to go to the bathroom and to eat once in a while."

"Because of your dad?"

"Probably. We lived in a shithole trailer that was falling apart. We were lucky to have electricity. Sometimes we didn't have heat or hot water." He rubs his hands up and down his face. "My dad had been abusing me since the moment I showed symptoms of color blindness. But again, it was better me than them."

"You were so brave."

He shakes his head. "I didn't feel like it. There were times when I was younger that I'd wet myself when he pulled in the driveway. I could tell what his mood was just by his body language. Those were the times Mom told me to change my clothes quickly and take Daisy to a nearby park to take pictures. Mom was the brave one. She always tried to protect us, no matter how deep her depression was."

"While you were trying to protect her."

He nods, his eyes sad.

"Didn't social services get involved?"

"Dad was a great actor. He always managed to convince them that everything was okay. He should've been a lawyer, the fucking bastard. You'd think social services would've known something was wrong just by looking at our house, but nothing ever came of their visits. Dad also told me that he'd hurt Mom and Daisy if I said anything to anyone, especially at school."

He shakes his head. "I'm sorry. I'm jumping all over the place."

"I'm getting the picture. Keep going."

"One day, my dad lost his driver's license. He was caught drunk driving, but it was his first offense, so he was able to avoid jail time. I still don't know how he paid for all the legal fees. As I got older and got jobs, he took my money. And he'd still threaten me with hurting Mom and Daisy. I'd do anything to protect them.

"Once I was older and could fight back, I slept in the same bedroom as Mom and Daisy to make sure he didn't do anything to them. He usually passed out on the couch or wherever he landed when he got home. Sometimes he didn't come home at all."

He takes a deep breath, and so do I. Bringing up these memories has to split his heart into two. I wonder where his father is today. I brush my fingers through his hair. He closes his eyes as if it's the best feeling. I keep doing it to make him relax.

"I knew he forced Mom to have sex. I heard it sometimes, and her crying afterward. I was so afraid he'd touch Daisy that way. There were times when he was drunk, and he'd look at her funny. My skin would crawl. I dreamed of a day that I could get them out of there. Really, I hoped he'd just leave one day and never come back. The only thing I had was my photography. It kept me going. And, as Mom encouraged me, I found it was something that took me to another world. I could find peace there for a little while."

"It seems to still do that for you. It's your outlet."

"It was. I think you're becoming my outlet. My vice." He pecks me on the lips, then pulls me even closer to him.

"So, fast-forward to one really bad day. A big fight broke out between my father and Mom. He hit her hard, and I couldn't take it anymore. I got in the middle. I told Mom to go back in her room because she didn't have the will to fight back anymore. I told Daisy to lock herself in the bathroom. She did."

"What were they fighting about?"

"Money. It was always money. Anyway, that day still replays in my mind. After a while, things cooled down and he left. I went to check on Mom." His body tenses up and he drops his head to my chest. His breathing increases. I have a feeling I know what he's going to say. He looks up at me, and his eyes are filled with tears. I wrap my arms around him as much as I can. My heart breaks.

"Tell me what happened."

He squeezes his eyes shut. A tear trickles down his cheek. "I went into her bedroom and found an empty bottle of pills next to her bed. She was already dead when I found her."

"Oh, Julius. I'm so sorry. I can't even imagine." I realize tears are streaming down my face. He looks at me and rubs them from my cheek. Still the protector.

"I should've been able to keep her safe."

"Julius, look at me." His pained eyes find mine. "It wasn't your fault. You have to know that. You can't blame yourself."

"In my head, I know you're right. But my heart will always think I should've done more. I should've seen the signs."

"What happened after that?"

"Dad went on a rampage. Kept saying she killed herself because of us, that we were worthless pieces of shit. There was no point in trying to convince him otherwise. But not too long after Mom died, our hell ended. Dad was riding his bicycle drunk and ran off the road. Broke his neck. He died instantly."

I want to say I'm sorry, but I'm not. The man was an asshole and deserved what he got. That poor family. I understand Daisy a little more now. And Julius a lot more.

"What happened to you and Daisy? How old were you?"

"She was fourteen and I was sixteen. My father's sister, Marie, came to the rescue. At first, they said they were going to have to split us up and send Daisy and me to different foster homes. Then my aunt found out what happened, and she took us under her wing. Dad had cut off all ties with her years before, so she'd had no idea of what was going on with us till then.

"She moved us in with her, and our lives changed for the better. It wasn't easy, but she had the patience of a saint. Her husband had died very young, so she'd never had kids and hadn't remarried. We became her kids.

"Once we settled down, she found an eye doctor who specialized in achromatopsia. My life drastically improved after that. She spoiled Daisy and me. She encouraged me to keep going with photography, and she's part of the reason we could afford to buy this place."

Just when I think they've reached a happy ending, he drops his head and groans.

"We were so fucked up, though. Just because we'd found a better life didn't mean we were mentally stable. Daisy had a really hard time, but I'm not going to get into the details. Let's just say my father had made her feel ugly and unworthy. So she decided tattoos would cover her ugliness. That's what she said when she started getting them. Then they became an obsession."

"Where's your aunt now?"

"Aunt Marie died from kidney failure. She was diabetic and we couldn't find a donor. So one after the other, the people we loved, died. Well, other than my father. I hated him." He paused and shook his head. "But you know what's horrible, Sky? I feel bad for saying that, even after all the suffering he put us through."

"That's because you have a heart. I see it in the way you take care of Daisy and Chance. I see it in how you act toward me. It's still in there, no matter how hard you've tried to protect it and keep it from feeling more."

This is major overload. My heart hurts for him. Emotions are pouring out of me through tears. I want to take all these memories away from him and give him the happiness and love he deserves. I can't imagine the weight he's carried all these years.

"I know some of this is confusing and I've jumbled it together. But this is me. This is why I am the way I am. I've been numb for years, but you're bringing me back to life." He stops, shaking his head.

"I don't know if I was ever truly alive. I've wasted so much time because of the past. I keep it quiet because I don't want to have to rehash it in interviews. I don't want pity from anyone. It's a private part of us, and Daisy doesn't need to be exposed to that either."

"You're still trying to protect her."

"I always will."

I nod. "Of course. It's who you are; it's in your

nature. I admire you. And look at how good you are with Chance."

He laughs. "Two peas in a pod. Both broken but he still finds joy. I should learn from him."

"Is there anything else you wanted to tell me? Nothing you told me makes me want to run out the door. If anything, it's made me want to be with you even more."

A slow and real smile appears on his face. "How did I get so lucky?" He kisses a trail from my chest up to my ear. I squirm because it tickles from his peach fuzz.

"I should be asking that question. I'm sleeping with the hottest guy I know, *and* he happens to be my favorite photographer. Nobody else could beat that."

His smile spreads across his face. "Thank you for understanding and accepting who I am. I don't understand why you'd want to be with someone who has so much baggage, but I'm glad you do."

"Everybody has a history, just some of it's worse than others. I can't explain it—I just know in my heart that you're who I want to be with." I shrug. "When you know you know. Some things can't be explained. I don't ever want to see anguish like that in your eyes again. Let me make you happy. Give *us* a chance."

And right on cue, Chance begins to scratch at the bedroom door.

"Time to get up," Julius says. He laughs and gets out of the bed, pulling me with him.

That laugh has become my favorite sound.

22

JULIUS

The last weeks have blown right by. Skylar's becoming a permanent fixture in my penthouse. Daisy gets along with her like she's the sister she never had. They even hang out together when I'm not home. Daisy is amazed, and so am I, on how easily I've let Sky into my life.

The atmosphere in the house has shifted. She has transformed our place into a home filled with laughter, happiness, and hope—something Daisy and I haven't had since Aunt Marie died. It took one person to make me hate my life when I was younger, and it took Skylar to make me love it now.

Daisy and I have had dinner a couple of times with Skylar's family. I was hesitant at first, but Skylar was cool about it. It's amazing how she understands and doesn't push me to do anything I don't want to. Some things I just need to take baby steps with, and that includes family situations and events.

To my surprise, we've always had a great time. Her

brothers, Christian and Drew, are cool. They don't drill me with questions or anything. From the stories they tell, it is easy to see that Jocelyn is the glue that keeps the family together. Skylar's lucky to have such warm, loving people to rely on. They already treat Daisy and me like we're part of their clan.

I have an interview with a magazine tomorrow morning. Daisy arranged it, but Skylar had to encourage me to do it. With her by my side, I feel like I can do anything. I've also agreed to attend the opening at the Mossi Krelo Gallery in February. It's only August... I can't think that far ahead, but Skylar says she'll go with me.

We're talking and planning things way in advance, something I haven't done much of. It sinks in a little more each day that she's not going anywhere. I guess I'm still a little insecure that she'll disappear someday because I've fucked up.

Which gets me to thinking about my future with her. I can't imagine being with another woman. I know I'm falling in love with her, but I haven't told her that yet.

Falling in love... with her...

I never said that to anyone. But she's aware of how much I care about her. Baby steps, even though we're on the fast track.

Saturday is going to be a huge test. Jocelyn and Christian are having a big barbecue at their house. I'll be meeting Skylar's mom and stepfather along with tons of other people. Daisy's coming too. She'll be my anchor. She's more social than I am. It's like she said to me after the last time we were with Skylar's family, maybe this is our chance to be a part of a big, happy family.

It's something I've always wanted, but I'm scared out of my mind about it. What if they don't like me? What if I don't fit in? What if I can't handle it at all?

I'm thirty-three years old and I sound so damn childish. I hate it.

But I'll suck it up because I'm going to do whatever makes Skylar happy.

"Hey, Cameron," I say, letting him through the door. Chance comes running from the kitchen. "Thanks again for watching Chance today. Sky's niece is really allergic to dogs. Her niece was sad I couldn't bring him, but I don't want to cause any problems."

"Happy to be here. You pay well." He laughs, then scratches Chance behind the ears as I close the door. "I'll take him to that dog park he likes. He'll be exhausted when you get home."

"I have no idea when we'll be back. If I survive this, it could be late." I swipe the sweat off my forehead as I walk to the kitchen.

"Man, you never get nervous," Cameron says from behind me. "Well, at least not in front of me. You'll do fine. Sky's really cool, so I can't imagine her family being any different. You've changed a lot. You might find it easier than you think." He pats me on the shoulder, then takes a seat at the kitchen island.

"I hope so. This'll be the first time I meet a woman's parents."

Cameron's eyebrows shoot up. "First time ever?"

I nod.

Since Cameron has been working with me more, we've become friends. He knows that I'm color-blind now. In fact, he's almost like a younger brother now. We joke around and sometimes he hangs out here after a shoot is finished. I'm not closed off like I was before. It's hard to believe this is my life right now.

Daisy walks out of the hallway, flipping through her phone.

"Hot damn! Look at you," Cameron expresses. "You are so hot in that yellow sundress, and I'm not even straight."

She twirls around and kisses him on the cheek. "Can you be a permanent fixture in this house? You make me feel so beautiful."

"You are, especially with those tats."

I clap my hands together. "Okay. Sky should be here any minute. Daisy, are you ready? Where's your cake?"

She walks over and rests her hand on my arm. "Look, I know you're nervous, Jules. I am too. But don't worry. If Sky has fallen in love with you—and she has—so will her parents. The rest of her family already adores you."

"What? What do you mean, she's in love with me?"

Daisy cocks an eyebrow and turns to Cameron. "Cameron, is Sky in love with my brother?"

"One hundred percent." He gives me a thumbs-up with a goofy grin.

"Did she tell you that?" My voice cracks, and I rub my hand through my hair for the sake of doing something.

"No, but we have eyes and it's obvious. But you want to know what's even more obvious? You're in love with her too." *Huh?*

I'm relieved when the doorbell rings.

"I'll get it," Daisy offers. Chance runs behind her because he probably knows Skylar's at the door. There's some chatter, barking, and laughing. Then Chance runs to me in the kitchen with a new toy in his mouth. He drops it on the floor to show me. I burst out laughing. It's a squirrel. Daisy follows and then Skylar.

I stop laughing because I can't breathe. She's beyond beautiful, and I haven't even seen what she's wearing. My eyes are locked on her sparkling ones, her perfect face and bare neck. Like always, and that's why I call her beautiful instead of Sky most of the time.

"You're spoiling Chance, Sky," Daisy complains. "He's not going to like us anymore. At least this one doesn't squeak."

Skylar sets her duffel bag to the side. "I just can't help it. He's so damn cute all the time. Besides, it's a squirrel. I had to get it; that's how Julius and I met." She ruffles Cameron's hair. "Hey, Cameron. Thanks for today." Then she finally looks at me and her face lights up.

She's in love with me. And I love her too. I've never felt so alive.

I walk up to her and take her face in my hands. "Hey, beautiful." My lips are on hers before she can answer. Daisy clears her throat, then I feel Skylar's lips curve up under mine.

"If you greet me like this every day, I'll be putty in your hands."

"I thought you already were."

"Oh, really?" She jabs me in the ribs playfully, then glances at Daisy and Cameron. "Since when is he such a smartass?"

"Since you came around. But I'd rather he be a funny smartass than his old broody self," Daisy responds.

Cameron nods in agreement. "Better get going before the smartass backs out."

Skylar laces her fingers through mine, then kisses the top of my hand. "You'll do fine. If it gets to be too much, we'll come back here and watch a movie in our pjs, since I'm staying over tonight." She pulls me toward the door.

"I like the staying over part. But I'll behave."

Daisy huffs with her cake in her hands and follows behind us.

"Cameron, you have our numbers. Have fun," I call out.

"Don't rush back," he jokes. "I make money on an hourly basis." Daisy and Skylar laugh as we walk out the door.

Okay. I've survived the first couple of hours and have to admit I'm having a good time. The weather is perfect, well for me anyway since it's overcast right now. Just like Skylar promised, her family has welcomed me and Daisy with open arms. Her mom and stepdad talked my ear off about art and my photography. I can see where Skylar's enthusiasm and personality come from. She has her mom's dark features and beauty too.

When Skylar said we were going to a barbecue, this isn't what I envisioned. This is more like a garden party you'd see in a magazine. There are several tables set up with fabric tablecloths with large floral arrangements adorning each one. Lanterns hang from the trees in the garden. There are even palm trees swaying in large planters scattered throughout the backyard. To the side is a smoker and a huge, sparkling gas grill. Kids have gravitated to a small pool area by the trees. And to top it off, there's a tent set up to cover the buffet. I'm surprised there's no DJ or band playing.

Will and Lacey are here, so I've been getting to know them better. I was pretty rude the first time I met them. Will's twin brother, Josh, is here too. When he saw Skylar, he picked her up off the ground and spun her around. They're always laughing and joking about something. I won't lie—I'm jealous. She's told me about him before and says he's a player. He tried to make the moves on her in St. Thomas, but she looks at him like a brother. I guess that should make me feel better. It does make me wonder, though, if she'd be better off with someone who's more outgoing.

Speak of the devil. "Having a good time?" Josh asks as he approaches me.

"Sure. They throw one hell of a barbecue."

"Yeah. So you're the lucky guy who took Sky off the market. Warning, don't get on her bad side. She doesn't take shit from anyone. She holds her ground and doesn't fall for any bullshit. Tough as nails but fun as hell." He's exactly right. "Have you ever been to the Hamptons?"

"No. I've never had the chance. I'd love to one day, though."

"You should visit with Sky before the summer's over. Bring Daisy along too. We can take you out on one of our boats."

Alert. I saw him talking to Daisy. She can take care of herself, but I can't help being protective. Especially if he's a player.

"Thanks for the invite. I'll talk to Sky about it. She has a tougher schedule than I do."

"Sky showed me your photo that Jocelyn and Christian bought from the gallery. You have amazing talent. You're perfect for Sky with her fascination with the arts. She's intimidating." We laugh at the same time.

"Tell me about it. She can describe my photos better than I can. She's amazing."

And she's mine.

Skylar approaches us carefully. "What are you gentlemen talking about?"

"You," we say in perfect unison. She turns on her heel and tries to walk away. I wrap my arm around her waist.

"You're not going anywhere. It's all good stuff. Josh says I'm a lucky man to have you."

She wraps her arms around me. "And what do you think of that?"

"I'd have to agree." I peck her lips. Suddenly there's a crowd.

"Excuse me. No public displays of affection, please," Daisy jokes. Jocelyn, Sophia, and Lacey come up from behind us.

"Sorry. Couldn't help it."

"Are you having fun, Julius?" Jocelyn asks. "I hope our family hasn't scared you. They scared me a little when I first met them." She leans in and whispers, "But don't tell them that."

"Same here," Sophia agrees quietly.

"Hey, that's my family you're talking about." Lacey swats their arms, then giggles.

"You sure know how to throw a party," I compliment Jocelyn. She beams.

"You have no idea," Lacey chimes in. "She's the party queen. I'm surprised she's not the wedding planner for Sophia and Drew's wedding."

"That's my sister, Tessa's, job," Sophia points out. "She's even more detail oriented than Jocelyn is. You should see the binder she has with her. We're including a lot of German traditions in the wedding. Well, we're trying to anyway."

"With a lot of German beer, I hope," Josh interrupts with a chuckle.

"Josh, she talked Chloe's ear off about the flowers. No wonder your sister escaped and went to another party," Sophia jokes.

"Well, I'm busy making your dress too," Jocelyn adds. "That's the most important thing. I'm under a lot of pressure to make it perfect. Which it will be." She starts to bite her nail, then self-consciously pulls her hand down. "Anyway, I need to socialize. We have so much food. Please eat, or I'll make you take home a doggie bag." And she's off, Sophia and Lacey following in her wake.

Maybe I'll sneak some for Chance, even though I shouldn't feed him too much human food.

"Daisy, want to get something to eat or drink?" Josh asks.

My body stiffens and Skylar squeezes my waist. "Yeah," she says. "Why don't you two check out the buffet. Daisy, your cake is almost gone already."

Daisy nods with a giant smile and walks away with Josh.

Skylar covers my mouth with her hand before I can comment. "Don't worry. He wouldn't do anything to piss me off or you. He's a flirt but a genuinely nice guy. Would that be so bad for Daisy?"

"It'll be hard for me to see her with any guy. No one will ever be good enough for her."

"Relax. She'll be—" My phone cuts her off. I pull it out of my pocket. *Huh.*

"It's Cameron. Let me go where it's quieter."

"Sure, I'll wait here for you."

I walk off to the side of the house. "Hey, Cameron. What's up?"

"Julius, you've got to come to the vet. Chance collapsed at the dog park. He's in with the doctor now. I can't do anything because I'm not his owner." He tries to explain, but I can't understand him very well. I don't like how his voice sounds, like it's worse than he's saying.

"Cameron, slow down. Text me where the vet is. I'll be there as soon as I can."

I rub my hands through my hair. *Chance is fine. He's a trooper.* I turn to find Skylar. She sees my face and reacts immediately.

"What's the matter? You're white as a ghost and you're rubbing your hand through your hair like you want to pull it out. You always do that when you're upset or nervous."

"I'm sorry, but I have to go. Cameron just called and said something's happened to Chance. They're at the vet. Where's Daisy?"

"I'll go with you."

"No. You stay here with your family. I'm sure he's fine." I look over her shoulder and search for Daisy in the crowd. "I'll take her with me."

"Are you sure? You're worrying me."

I kiss her forehead. "Yes. Stay here and enjoy the party. I'll call you when we know what happened."

"Okay, but just so you know, I'm not happy about this. I want to go with you." I shake my head and she sighs. "All right. I'll go get Daisy and tell Jocelyn and Christian that you're leaving."

"Tell them I'm sorry we have to go so soon. I'll be out front."

Ten minutes later, the taxi arrives and Daisy and I are on our way to the vet.

"I'm sure it's nothing major." I keep saying it, trying to convince myself it's true. But I keep getting text messages from Cameron asking when we'll be there. "He'll be fine."

Daisy agrees with me, holding my hand. "Chance has survived the worst… He can get through this too."

I pull my hand away and start rubbing my thigh. If anything happens to him, I know I'll break.

We finally arrive, and Cameron's pacing in front of the building. I throw money at the driver and jump out of the car. Once he sees us, he runs up to us.

"How is he?"

"I—I don't know," he responds with a shaky voice. "They won't tell me anything. They're waiting for you."

I run through the entrance and talk to the reception-ist. She takes me to a separate room. Daisy comes in a few minutes later without Cameron. After speaking to him alone and seeing how upset he was, she told him to go home. She'll call him later with an update.

"What the fuck could've happened?" I growl. I pace the room. The receptionist wouldn't tell me anything. Just as I'm about to rip the door off the frame, someone else comes in.

"Where's Chance? What's happened to him? I want to see him."

"Hi. I'm Dr. Janskin. Are you Julius Levi?" He reaches out his hand to shake mine.

"Yes." I shake his hand and probably squeeze it a little too hard. "Where's Chance?"

"Has anyone told you what happened?"

"Just that he collapsed!" I exclaim with frustration.

"Julius, settle down," Daisy urges. "Let him talk."

"From what your friend told me," the doctor says, "they were at a dog park. Chance was running around like normal, then suddenly he collapsed. When he woke up, he was very lethargic and whimpering. Cameron brought him here immediately. I took some bloodwork and did an X-ray."

"And? What's the problem?" I want to shake the information out of him.

"He has a large tumor on his liver and one on his spleen. The one on the liver ruptured while he was playing. His liver is severely damaged, and he has a lot of internal bleeding."

"So will he be okay? Can I see him?"

"I'm sorry, Mr. Levi." He's silent for a moment. My heart stops. "There's nothing we can do. His vitals are dropping, and he's in a lot of pain. We've given him a high dose of painkillers." I hear the doctor say that he's recommending we put Chance to sleep.

I stop listening. He doesn't stop talking.

"Mr. Levi, is that what you want to do? I need your consent before I proceed."

I close my eyes and pray that this is a dream and I'll wake up any second. But I don't. This is reality. Why? Why him? A hand covers my shoulder, and I twitch.

"Julius, you know what we have to do." Daisy's voice cracks. "We can't let him suffer. It's the best thing for him." I yank my shoulder away.

"Mr. Levi, what should we do?" He asks very slowly, but directly.

It takes everything in me not to break down. I can hardly breathe. But I nod to the doctor because I can't speak. Daisy picks up on it, and answers for me. He explains the process and tells us we can be in the room with him. They'll take us to him in a minute. After the doctor exits, I fall to my knees. Daisy wraps her arms around me, and we cry together.

I don't know how much time passes while we wait. Our phones have been ringing nonstop and I know it's Skylar. We turn them off.

The doctor returns and tells us to follow him. He explains the procedure again. "He's in here. We've made him as comfortable as possible. Talk to him. I don't know if he'll respond because of the medicine, but he'll know you're both here."

He opens the door. I squeeze my eyes shut and tears fall down my cheeks. Behind me, Daisy gasps. I open my eyes and see him on the table. He's facing the door, but he doesn't respond to our presence.

The world spins out of control. My body shakes like a leaf as I cross the room. There are two chairs placed next to the table, one at the head and one at the side. I stop.

Daisy wraps her arm around me and nudges me forward. I stand behind the chair and look at his little body lying on a blanket. His chest moves up and down slowly. How could he be dying? Hours ago he was running around like he always did. There had been no signs that he was sick.

She pulls out the chair for me. My heart pounds in my chest, and I sit down slowly. She moves to the other seat at the head of the table. My hands shake profusely as I reach over to pet my dog. My friend. Daisy strokes the side of his neck.

"I'm here, Chance. Daisy is too." *Wake up. Please wake up.*

The doctor comes in and puts something in the IV to start the procedure. Daisy and I keep stroking his head, his body. I rest my chin on my arm near his face, and start talking to him. Telling him how great he is and how much we'll miss him. Suddenly, he raises his head and licks my face. A whimper follows from him. My head pops up. *He's saying goodbye!* I look into his eyes and watch them slowly close again. He's still. The doctor waits a minute, checks his vitals, then pronounces he's gone.

Tears pour out like a waterfall. Daisy wraps her arm around my shoulders again and cries with me. I hug him one more time.

"Chance, buddy. Wherever you are, I hope you're running through long fields with all four legs now... cheeks and tongue flapping in the wind. You'll never hurt again. You were the best. I love you."

The doctor leads us out of the room, and we make arrangements for cremation.

I want to run to Skylar.

But I don't think I ever will again.

23

SKYLAR

"He won't answer his phone. Daisy isn't either. This isn't good." I scrub my eyebrows so fiercely there's probably nothing left. Lacey rubs my back.

"Why don't you sneak out of here. Go see what's going on. Maybe they're at home."

"If they are, why haven't they called me? Something bad has to have happened. And if it did, Julius will be a mess. That dog was like a son to him. To me too."

He's going to push me away.

"Go. Get out of here. I'll tell everyone what happened. A bunch of us are crashing here tonight. Anything happens and you need to talk, you come straight here. Understand?"

"I hope Jocelyn will be okay with that."

"You're talking about Jocelyn. She'd be waiting for you on the front doorstep." I let out a light chuckle.

"I love you." Lacey pulls me in for a hug. "I'll call you."

"Good luck. I hope it's just a misunderstanding."

Me too.

I raise my finger to Julius's doorbell but hesitate. What if it's the worst-case scenario—which my gut is saying it is. I don't think they're going to welcome me with open arms. Daisy might, but not Julius. We might not have known each other for long, but I can read him like a book.

I suck it up and ring the bell.

I press my ear against the door, hoping to hear Chance's nails scrape along the floor… but silence ensues. Maybe they aren't at home. I press the button again. Finally, the door opens, and it's Daisy with makeup smeared down her face.

I cover my mouth with both hands. She jumps into my arms and cries. *Oh no!* "What happened, Daisy? Where's Chance?"

She pulls away from me and wipes the tears off her cheeks. She steps to the side so I can walk in, then closes the door.

"Daisy, what the hell is going on? It's been hours, and you guys haven't answered any of my calls or messages. I've been worried sick."

She walks me into the kitchen and, between sobs, unloads everything that has happened. Chance is gone. Gone! Next to my foot on the floor is the squirrel I gave him today. My own tears flow. How can things change so quickly?

I blow my nose and push my hair away from my

face. My lungs expand to take in a deep breath that I desperately need. "Where's Julius?" Fear skates through me.

"I don't know if you want to see him. He's a mess and I don't know what to do. He went straight to his room when we got home. He hasn't come out since."

"I need to see him… be there for him."

"He's going to shut us out. Both of us. I don't care how much he loves you, he'll push you away. It's what he does." *He loves me?* He's never said it.

"I have to try. I love him too, Daisy."

"I know." A mask of pity covers her face. "But I don't know if it's enough. The more he loves someone, the harder he pushes them away when something bad happens. Don't let him."

I nod and close my eyes, trying to give myself a pep talk. I'm a tough chick from Boston and I tell it like it is. And he likes that about me, right?

I walk out of the kitchen and notice Chance's toys splayed throughout the open living space. My chest tightens. If I feel like I'm going to lose it, I can only imagine what Julius is battling. This is a situation I've never faced before.

A few footsteps later, I'm standing in front of his bedroom door. I push my ear against it to hear if there is any movement. *Silence.* My body quivers as I tap on the door. *Silence.*

"Go on in," Daisy urges from behind me. What if it's locked?

The knob turns without stopping and a small sense of relief swirls through my body. I push it open slightly, preparing myself for what I might see. The lights aren't on, but the late day sun shines through the window to the left. He's sitting on the lounge chair in the corner of his room. His body is completely limp. His hair is disheveled and his shirt is opened, revealing his chest. My heart breaks a little bit more and I'm afraid to breathe in the still silence. I close the door behind me.

He doesn't acknowledge that someone's in his room.

"Julius, it's me." I approach him cautiously. *Silence.* I kneel down in front of him, but not too close. "I'm so sorry." My voice cracks.

His heaving chest grabs my attention. My breath rushes out of me when I see his tear-covered face. I want to pull him in my arms, but there's a wall of negative energy around him. I look into his eyes but they reflect only emptiness. There's no love or warmth there. It's as if he's erased me from his heart.

"Leave," he says bitterly. "Go back to your happy fucking family." I flinch at his evil tone.

Hang on, Sky! I tell myself. *Remember, he's hurting.*

But my sadness turns to rage. He's not going to shut me out or use me as his punching bag. I won't let him. I want to take all his pain away—I could at least try—but I know he won't let me. He's closed himself off, and I don't know if he'll ever come back to me.

"I don't want you or anybody here." His voice is flat and hard.

"Julius, we all loved Chance. We're all hurting right along with you. Let me help you get through this."

He jumps up from the chair, making me fall back on

my hands. "I don't want your fucking help... I don't want anybody's help. I just want to be left alone."

I stand up swiftly. "Well, thanks for your honesty, but it's bullshit. You do need us. You need me. I won't let you ruin what we have."

"There is no us, Skylar. I have nothing to offer you. If I wouldn't have left him today, he'd still be alive!" *Skylar*... Not Sky.

"That's not true, and you know it. He was sick and if it didn't happen today, it would've happened another day. With or without you there."

"I don't care. I shouldn't have gone with you today. I knew it—the moment I let myself be happy, I knew something would destroy it. And it has. I can't love you the way you should be loved. Find someone like Josh who has less baggage. I can't make you happy when I'm miserable. I'll only drag you down with me, and that's not fair to you."

"I don't want Josh or any other man. I want you!"

He shakes his head and stalks to the window. He props his hands on the sill and stares outside.

"Julius! Look at me, damn it."

"I told you to leave. I'm better off alone. This crippling feeling in my chest isn't worth it. The pain's too much to bear again. I'm better off being numb."

I walk over and pull on his arm so he'll look at me. I'm mad. I *am* that girl from Boston, who tells it like it is. And he's gonna hear it.

"You didn't learn a damn thing from Chance. It's so sad. You gave him a new life, a better life. He took advantage and lived it to the fullest every second of the day. He was broken, but he didn't care because he had you—the one person who loved him unconditionally and set him free.

"And this tree on your back. The tree of life." I scoff. "What a load of shit. It's supposed to mean rebirth. A new chance at life. What did you say? Positivity and bright future? Right. You weren't reflecting any of that when I first met you. Nor did it mean anything in your past, apparently. Not even after your aunt took you both in. You never really lived like that. But it started to show when you met me. I saw it there."

He rakes his hands roughly through his hair, then looks away.

"I can't do this, Skylar. Why can't you let me be?"

"Because when you hurt, I hurt. Why does Chance's death mean you have to throw us away? His death is a reminder that life can change in a second. You have the chance to be happy with me. I love you, Julius."

His head swings in my direction again. A sign of life flashes in his eyes, but then, as quickly as it came, it's gone again. Well, I'm not done.

"You heard me. I love you. Yes, I'm saying it out loud, and I know it scares the shit out of you. It does me too. But it's the best damn feeling in the world, and that outweighs the fear. I love you for everything you are, baggage and all. I love how you take care of Daisy and how you adored Chance. How you want to help Cameron. You always want people to think you're a big tough guy with no feelings, but that's so far from the truth. You have a heart of gold. I've seen it. I've seen *you* without your wall up." He steps around me and walks toward the door. I follow him. He's going to hear me out.

"The problem is, you don't see me. You claim you do, but if you did, you'd already know how much I love you. Every action or just how I look at you should show you that. I want all of you. Even with the trust issues I have, I'm willing to take the chance on us. Even if I end up hurt in the end! But let's not hurt each other. Let's build a new life together."

He swings the door wide open.

"I said I can't do this. I'm sorry."

I force my tears back and bite my lip. I walk out the door, and then I turn to him for the final time. "You have one life, Julius. Learn from Chance and take advantage of the time you have on this earth. Everyone has the right to be happy. Find what makes you happy and hold onto it, even if it's not me. You'll regret it in the end if you don't. But remember that I love you. Sometimes that's all you need."

Then I turn my back on him and walk away. I hear the door close quickly behind me. Daisy sits on the couch in the living room staring into space. I pick up the squirrel from the floor and place it on the table near the door. Then I leave without saying goodbye. And that's when the heavy tears flow.

Jocelyn opens her front door and ushers me inside. Lacey, Sophia, and Tessa come from around the corner. I called Lacey once I could breathe again and told her what happened. Lacey gets to me first and envelops me in her arms.

"I'm so sorry, Sky," she says.

"I should have known," I reply. "My perfect track record and all."

"Men." Lacey huffs, and I join her in a half-laugh. "Why does this feel like a repeat of you all comforting me about Will after our trip to St. Thomas?"

I pull away. "Because love sucks? The big difference here is, I don't think there'll be a happy ending for me. Remember what I always say about myself? Forever hopeful, but always let down."

Jocelyn rubs my arm, then closes the door. "Aw, honey. I'm sure you'll work things out. Come on, the men are still here but they're outside smoking cigars. We can chat inside without polluting our lungs."

She leads us into the living room, and I have to smile. Her house is always so cozy and inviting. The large coffee table has snacks and wine ready for us. Candles are lit everywhere. The couches are big and comfortable. It feels like it's midnight, but it's only ten. I'm so exhausted, I could fall asleep on one of them right now.

Lacey, Sophia, and I settle on the couches, while Jocelyn and Tessa sit on the floor in front of the table. Glasses are filled and their attention is all on me.

Suddenly, I sit up. "Sophia, where are your parents?"

"They're back at the hotel. Tessa's going to stay at our place tonight."

Tessa sits forward, an earnest expression on her face.

"Sky, would you like me to leave? I don't want to intrude." Her voice is so cute with her German accent. I spoke to her a lot today, and I already feel she's part of the clan. Sophia talks about her all the time too.

"No, not at all. I'm sure Lacey updated you all on what happened with Chance after I called a little while ago." I pick up a glass of white wine and drink it like it's water. Big swallows ward off the tears. The girls all say they're sorry and drip with sympathy.

"So what exactly happened with Julius when you were at his place?" Lacey asks. "I mean, you told me about Chance and how Julius was upset, but—what really happened?"

"As soon as Daisy told me that Chance was gone, I knew Julius would push me away. He's got so much baggage, so many losses in his life. And that's exactly what he did. Even after I told him I'm in love with him. Damn it! I know I fell fast—we've only known each other for a little while, but it's real. For him too, and—"

I look up and realize they're all staring at me, eyes wide and mouths open. "What?"

"For someone who never thought that love at first sight was possible for her, you've sure changed your tune," Lacey answers.

"Of course, we already knew," Jocelyn chimes in. "Even at the opening, you could see the spark. And today, fireworks were flying everywhere. You'd think it was the fourth of July. His actions showed us all we needed to know. And you know what they say, actions speak louder than words. He's in love with you too." She reaches over and refills my glass. The rest of them nod in agreement.

"Well, he claims he's not." I let my body sink into the couch.

"He said that?" Sophia presses, reflecting doubt.

"No. Not really." I repeat what he said to me. Then I stick up for him. "Listen, he's had a bad past. I can't tell you what he's experienced because it's too private. But I understand why he's pushing me away. And right now, nothing's going to change his mind. I'm not going to beg."

"I guess I understand that," Lacey says. "But the big question is, are you willing to deal with all the stuff that comes along with him?"

"Yes, because even with his heavy baggage, he's the best man I know. And I'll always love him, even if he doesn't find his way back to me."

He's got to fight for his future. I can't do that for him.

24

JULIUS

It's been a week and two days since Chance died and I pushed Skylar away. My life is emptier than it has ever been before. Even with all the shit I've dealt with in the past.

I've tried to crawl back into my old routine, but it doesn't feel right. Chance isn't here anymore. He doesn't need to be taken for a walk or be fed or be played with. Skylar somehow also became a part of that routine. Taking lazy walks with Chance after work had become our favorite part of the day. It was like we were already a family and Chance was our son. It was only for a short time, but I miss it like hell.

I miss *her* like hell. The horrible weight on my chest isn't just because I've lost Chance. It's because I've lost her too. Well, I didn't lose her. I pushed her away. She did nothing wrong. She did everything right, and I let her down. It's all my fault.

She left her duffel bag here the day Chance died. When I finally came out of my room, I promptly tripped over it. Daisy stuck it right in front of my door. On purpose, I'm sure. I put it in my room and left it there. Skylar hasn't called to say she wants it back, and I haven't had the nerve to call her. I've asked Daisy to return it for me, but she refused. She keeps saying it's my problem to deal with… along with a bunch of other things I don't want to hear.

The bag has been staring at me every day. I want to open it but every time I do, I find something to distract me until I don't anymore. And then I picked it up. All it took was opening the zipper to be surrounded by a cloud of her vanilla scent. And then I knew.

She was right about everything she said to me before I shoved her out my door. I'm ashamed of myself and how weak I am. Yes, I had to grieve. But I could have grieved with her.

I went to the gallery a couple of days ago and watched her through the window. She was with a customer, so she didn't see me. And then… she smiled at the woman, and my heart broke in two. She was smiling, but her smile didn't reach her eyes. *Have I extinguished her light?* It's all I can think of.

I'd do anything to make her smile again. The one that lit me up every time I saw it. Wait a second! An idea suddenly pops into my head. With a spike of energy swimming through my veins, I open my laptop and search through my photos.

I yank my mobile out of my pocket to call Cameron. He showed up here a couple of nights after Chance died. We talked a lot about what happened, and I also opened up about Sky when he asked me about her. He didn't say anything that I hadn't already heard from Daisy regarding pushing Sky away. When he left, I told him I'd be in touch about work. I call his number.

He answers on the first ring. "Hey, Julius. How are you doing?"

We chat for a few minutes, then I get to the point. "So the main reason I'm calling is that I need help on a project. It's to win Sky back. Are you in?"

"Fuck yeah."

"Good. Come by at nine tomorrow morning." He agrees and we disconnect the call.

Next, I text Daisy and ask her for Monica Morrison's phone number.

Skylar was *wrong*. I *do* see her and I'm going to prove it. I've seen her all along.

This had better work.

25

SKYLAR

Monica called me the other day and said she'd be in the city for some art event. She wants to meet at the gallery today. It's Sunday morning and I'm tired. I'm pretty much tired of everything right now.

Yesterday was the last day of Julius's exhibit. Monica wants to help me take everything down and discuss the next photographer's exhibit and opening before she heads back to Boston. On top of that, we need to go through the resumes we've received for the open position.

My days have consisted of me submerging myself in work as a distraction. Ironically—no, unfortunately— I'm surrounded by Julius's photographs while I'm at work. The name *Julius Ariti* has been on constant repeat in my head as I try to replace my memories of Julius Levi with those early ones, before I knew who he really was. When that didn't work, I just hid in my office until someone entered the gallery.

I haven't heard a peep from him. It's been torture

not to hear his sexy voice, to feel his soft lips against mine, or to see his gorgeous face. I think what I miss the most are the lazy walks we'd take with Chance, hand in hand. He made us laugh so much. We had become three peas in a pod instead of two.

Sometimes, at odd moments, I've felt like he was near me. I even thought I saw him out the corner of my eye a few times. But when I search for him, he's never there. Just blank faces in the crowds around me. Wishful thinking. Daisy only communicates with me through email. And as soon as we take down this exhibit, I won't have any contact with her either.

I glance at my phone and purse my lips. Monica doesn't usually get on my nerves, but this weekend she has. She sent me about ten messages yesterday and a couple more already this morning. Now she's wondering where I am—I'm only two minutes late! I text back that I'm on my way and jam my phone into my pocket. I can't deal. Man, I'm in a shitty mood today.

Before long, I can see the door to the gallery. Monica's there, waiting impatiently. She sees me and steps outside with her purse like she's leaving.

"Hey, Monica. Are you going somewhere?"

"I broke something, and I need to go buy a new one. I'll be back in a little while."

"Um. Okay. I'll be here." She waves and hurries off.

That's weird. But you know what? I don't really care. I shake my head and shove open the door. I pause to enjoy the cool air that greets me. Then the damn buzzer goes off, pissing me off even more. I toss my bag on the front desk, then turn around to see if Monica has done anything with Julius's pictures yet.

I fall back onto the desk and blink several times. Each photo of his that was hanging in the front has been replaced with a black and white photo. Of me.

I don't understand. Is this why Monica left?

I push off the desk, my heart pounding. My legs feel like rubber, but I make it to the first picture. My mouth falls open. It's from the shoot. He said he was going to touch up the pictures and show them to me when he was done. And he did show me a few, but not this one. It's only of my face. It's a good thing because I'd be pissed if one of the full body shots was displayed out in the open. Not that I'm high on myself, but I look beautiful. And sexy. And happy. I walk to the next one. It's also from the shoot, when he was standing above me and I was looking up at him. A smile forms on my face, but my chest hurts from missing him. I'll never forget the way Julius made me feel that night.

I step around the corner to see if there are more. A screech leaves my mouth, and I come to an abrupt stop. "Julius!"

He's standing about six feet away, watching me intently. My stomach swirls in delight like it always does when he's near. I want to jump in his arms, but I don't move.

"Hi, Sky," he says with a weary but sweet grin.

"Monica knew about this?" *Of course she did.*

He nods. "Some other elves helped too. They're big fans of yours." I open my mouth to respond, but he raises his hand. "Wait. Let me say what I came here to say first."

I nod and suck my lower lip into my mouth to prevent myself from smiling.

"Before I pushed you out of my life, you said I didn't see you. At that moment of time, you were right. I couldn't see anything or anyone because I only saw darkness. I didn't want to believe you loved me." He steps closer and points to the wall to the right. "If you look through these pictures, it'll become clear that I did see you."

I glance at what he's referring to and gasp. My hand covers my mouth. Back here too, the walls are covered with photos of me. Not just from the shoot. These pictures are also only of my face. He's always got a camera on him, but when did he take these?

"I want you to know exactly how I see you—through my eyes. You think everyone's blinded by your curves. Don't get me wrong, you're the most beautiful woman I know. But that's just a benefit. No matter what we were doing, I could see your different moods, your kindness, your positivity, intelligence, and confidence, and the love you show for others… and me. Half the time, you didn't even know I was taking your picture. I know that sounds kind of creepy."

"*Pfft.* You think?" I walk down the line of pictures with my arms wrapped around myself, then stop at one. He approaches me, but still keeps his distance. I don't want him to stay away, but maybe it's better this way. At least I try to convince myself of that. He points to the photo I've stopped at.

"That one's my favorite. I took it the first night we spent together. You were sleeping so peacefully."

"I remember. I woke up to you watching me." I eye him. "Speaking of creepy."

The side of his mouth quirks up. "The idea of taking pictures of you like this came to me not long after we met. There's a light that radiates from you. It fascinates me. I think Chance saw it too. But you inspired me to take pictures of living things—people, not structures. I used to treat the models like objects, not humans. You've changed my perspective. My bodyscapes—those photos are distant. They're beautiful, but they lack life. You bring life to my photos. No, you bring life to everything you touch… including me."

He points to the tiny smile I'm wearing in the picture. "That's the face I want to wake up to every morning. I want to make you smile like that every night before you fall asleep and every morning when you wake up."

"Julius. I'm speechless." I want to reach out to him, but I stay where I am. I don't want him to stop talking.

He takes my hands in his, and I melt. That instant heat and electricity that I became familiar with when he touched me is still there.

"Sky, even though I see you only in black and white, I see your different colors better than anyone else. I lived more in the short time we were together than I have my entire life. I felt happiness, excitement, and hope when I was with you. You were and still are my addiction. Just like I loved Chance unconditionally, you loved me like that too. Broken pieces and all.

"Chance died, and it was a repeat of my past. I couldn't prevent it. I wasn't able to save my mom, I couldn't help my aunt when she died, then Chance... I didn't want to feel anymore."

I nod my head. "I know. But what made you change your mind?"

"Easy. The silence. You and Chance filled my life with constant noise. I could sit and listen to you talk and laugh for hours. The way you interacted with Daisy like she's your own sister. How you played with Chance and spoiled him rotten. You introduced Daisy and me to your family. That little glimpse at the barbecue made me want a family with you. If Chance hadn't banged into you, we might never have met that day in the park."

He presses our clasped hands against his chest. "Photography has always been my dream. It's what I lived for. But it's not anymore."

"It's not?" I move closer to him and glance at his perfect pink lips, then into his glimmering beautiful eyes.

"No. It's not. You are. We are. I was a complete asshole. I know that, and I know I don't deserve you. But let me show you how much I love you and not just through pictures."

I pull my head back with astonishment. "What— what did you just say?"

He smiles warmly. "I love you, Sky. I do. You're the love of my life. I can't go back to the way I lived before I met you. Please give me another chance."

My heart swells in my chest. "Julius, neither one of us is perfect alone, but when we're together, we're more than perfection. It'll take a lot more than this before I give up on us." I wrap my arms around his neck. "Can I have a kiss now? Or do you have something else to say?"

He cups my cheeks with his hands, then hovers his lips over mine. "Not until I hear those three magical words again. The words I never thought would come from your beautiful mouth."

"I love you, Julius. And I always will."

"Music to my ears."

Then he captures my lips with his, proving to me that this is exactly where we're supposed to be.

Thanks, Chance.

The End

Don't forget to check out Daisy and Josh's story in Maple Trees and Maybes.

BOOKS BY KRISTINA BECK

Collide Series

Lives Collide

Dreams Collide

Souls Collide

Collide Series Box Set

Four Seasons Series

Snowflakes and Sapphires – Winter

Passions and Peonies – Spring

Colors and Curves – Summer

Maple Trees and Maybes – Autumn

Standalone Novels

Into Thin Air

Love Ever After Anthology

ACKNOWLEDGMENTS

What a crazy year it's been so far. And boy was it hard to write this book. As COVID-19 spread around the world, it changed how we lived our lives. Suddenly I went from having quiet mornings alone when I could focus and write, to a full house twenty-four hours a day, seven days a week. My priorities had to shift.

I'm very thankful for the time I've had with my family. My husband has always traveled a lot and worked long hours. To have him home with us all the time was a dream. I'm not a fan of homeschooling because I'm not a good teacher. Trying to keep three kids in check was not easy and caused a lot of stress in the house. Hopefully the next school year will be back to normal. Through it all, we were blessed with good health and we're closer as a family.

So to get back to what I was trying to say. It took me a lot longer to write this book because the motivation wasn't there. I was tired, stressed, and sad about what was going on around the world. But once I typed the last words, I was more than ecstatic that I finally finished it. It's a lot longer than I planned, but it had to be with the story I was trying to tell.

My beta readers were so patient with me and motivated me along the way. I was so excited to get such positive feedback from them. Thank you, Ilona Ahrens, Rachel Childers, Lisa Hemming, and Jamie Buck. You're the best and I love that we are a team!

I had to research a bit about running a gallery. I turned to my lovely friend, Susanne Jeffs. She worked in a gallery for several years so she was able to give me some helpful hints. Thank you!

The book cover wasn't easy to design either. I searched so many image sites for ideas and nothing would work. I wasn't sure if it was the mood I was in at the time. Finally I found something and it took off from there. Jody Kaye, I can't thank you enough for your patience. I know it wasn't easy. We both worked so hard on this one. The final cover came out even better than I imagined. Thank you so much!

My editing team makes my life easier because I know how reliable they are. Rachel Overton, you are a champion. Even when you were sick, you pushed to edit this book anyway. I can't thank you enough. Helen Pryke, thanks for always finding the time within your busy schedule to work with me. I always know my books are in good hands.

Even though I should know how to format my own books by now, working with Rik Hall makes it so much easier. I send off the manuscript and within hours it's sent back to me in a perfect package. Rik, you're awesome.

Chance wasn't a fictional character. My sister, Betsy, had a three-legged dog named Chance. He brought her never-ending joy for the short time he was with her family. Sadly, he was also sick and had to be put to sleep. Thanks for making my sister happy. She loved you so much.

As always, hugs and kisses to my husband and kids. Thanks for giving me space when I needed it during these last months. I know it's not easy to always hear me say, "I have to work." To my oldest daughter, Sarah, I love it that you read my books and enjoy them. At least that's what you say. It melts my heart.

To my readers, thanks for sticking by me for the last three years. You keep me going when I find myself in doubt. Any interaction with my readers makes me happy for the rest of the day. I promise I'll do my best with every book I write.

Many blessings to everyone during this hard time in 2020. We need to stick together and hope that some normalcy finds us again. Hug your friends and family, and always let them know how much you love them. Stay safe and healthy. We can get through this.

ABOUT THE AUTHOR

Kristina Beck was born and raised in New Jersey, USA, and lived there for thirty years. She later moved to Germany and now lives there with her German husband and three children. She is an avid reader of many genres, but romance always takes precedence. She loves coffee, dark chocolate, power naps, flowers, and eighties movies. Her hobbies include writing, reading, fitness, and forever trying to improve her German-language skills.

To receive updates on her new releases, sales, and book signings, signup for her newsletter on her website or follow her on social media.

www.kristinabeck.com

f facebook.com/krissybeck73

⊙ instagram.com/krissybeck96

ⓐ amazon.com/author/kristinabeck

BB bookbub.com/authors/kristina-beck

g goodreads.com/kristina_beck

Made in the USA
Middletown, DE
03 December 2022